THE SIEGE OF THE ALAMO

SOLDIERING IN THE TEXAS REVOLUTION

THE SIEGE OF THE ALAMO

SOLDIERING IN THE TEXAS REVOLUTION

Susan Provost Beller

 Twenty-First Century Books • Minneapolis

To all the Americans who have given their lives in service to create and defend the United States

Title page image: This plaque at the Alamo commemorates the men who died defending it in 1836.

Twenty-First Century Books
A division of Lerner Publishing Group, Inc.
241 First Avenue North
Minneapolis, MN 55401 U.S.A.

Website address: www.lernerbooks.com

Library of Congress Cataloging-in-Publication Data

$33.26
9/08

Beller, Susan Provost, 1949–
     The siege of the Alamo : soldiering in the Texas revolution / by Susan Provost Beller.
         p.   cm. — (Soldiers on the battlefront)
     Includes bibliographical references and index.
     ISBN 978–0–8225–6782–0 (lib. bdg. : alk. paper)
     1. Alamo (San Antonio, Tex.)—Siege, 1836. 2. Alamo (San Antonio, Tex.)—Siege, 1836—
Personal narratives. 3. Texas—History—Revolution, 1835–1836. 4. Texas—History—Revolution,
1835–1836—Personal narratives. 5. Soldiers—Texas—Biography. 6. Texas. Militia—Biography.
I. Title.
F390.B44 2008
976.4'03—dc22   2007001720

Manufactured in the United States of America
1 2 3 4 5 6 — JR — 13 12 11 10 09 08

Contents

"I shall never surrender or retreat."

—William Barret Travis, 1836

PROLOGUE

On March 6, 1836, just at daybreak, about six thousand Mexican *soldados* (soldiers), under the command of General Antonio López de Santa Anna, attacked the Alamo, a small fort defended by fewer than two hundred men. Most of the Alamo defenders were Texians (Americans who had settled in the Mexican province of Texas). Some of them had just arrived. One, the frontiersman David Crockett, was already a legend. In less than an hour, all the defenders were dead, though each had taken six or seven soldados to the grave. Within days, this small battle became a legend. It is so much of a legend that it is hard to find the real history hidden within it. Santa Anna was more than willing to see himself portrayed as the successful conqueror. His soldados were poor, illiterate peasants who left no stories to tell their side of the fight. The defenders all died within the walls of the fort. Historians have spent more than 170 years trying to reconstruct that short hour to understand why it still captures the imagination so long after the event.

Visitors to the Alamo find only a small mission church in the middle of the bustling city of San Antonio, Texas. It is quite a small

The mission church *(right)* found at the Alamo seems very small compared to the bustling city of San Antonio, Texas, that surrounds it. Many visitors come to the Alamo each year.

monument to have had such a large impact on U.S. history and memory. It appears small, partly because only the mission church portion of the original fort survives. But even if the entire fort existed, it still would not seem very big. It was smaller than the forts used in the French and Indian War (1754–1763) and the American Revolution (1775–1783). It was smaller than Fort McHenry, the fortress whose gallant defense gave us our national anthem, "The Star Spangled Banner," during the War of 1812 (1812–1815). At the time of the siege, the Alamo had been used as a military fortress for about thirty-five years. It was essentially a large courtyard surrounded by stone walls. The walls were only twelve feet high at their highest point, easy for an enemy to scale.

The Alamo defenders were also small in number. More Americans were killed or wounded in most other battles in U.S. history. Only twenty-six years later, at the Battle of Antietam during the Civil War (1861–1865), twenty times as many people were killed in a one-day fight. The Alamo defenders were not even victorious in their fight. They were heroes because they fought to the end, even though they lost.

This small site does manage to tell a large story. It is a story of the desperate heroism that characterized a critical moment in U.S. history.

The interior of the mission church building at the Alamo serves as a museum. The little building tells a large story about the independence and statehood of Texas.

This one story came to represent the larger story of the settlement of the United States as the growing nation expanded westward. This expansion was called Manifest Destiny—the American belief that the United States had the right to all the territory from sea to sea.

The Alamo's impact on U.S. history is itself an amazing tale. The phrase "Remember the Alamo" resounded through time, becoming "Remember the Maine" in the Spanish-American War (1898) and "Remember Pearl Harbor" in World War II (1939–1945). Even President Franklin D. Roosevelt, rallying Americans to heroism in the darkest days of World War II, evoked its memory. Quoting the commander of the Alamo, William Barret Travis, Roosevelt said, "Travis' message—I shall never surrender or retreat—is a good watchword for each and every one of us today."

Small site, large story, and increased significance through time have kept the Alamo fresh and alive for more than 170 years. This is quite a tribute to a battle that did not even take place in what was then the United States but instead in a province of Mexico. Still, the siege of the Alamo is a U.S. story well worth telling.

> "[Texas] will be the best, the brightest star in the Mexican constellation."
>
> —Stephen F. Austin, 1830

CHAPTER ONE

THE NEED TO MOVE WEST

From the colonial period until the late nineteenth century, U.S. history is marked by growth and movement. One of the grievances that led to the American Revolution was that the British king prohibited colonists from moving west of the Appalachian Mountains. After the Revolution, soldiers were given grants of land, called bounties, west of the mountains as payment for their military service. Some of the soldiers moved west with their families to claim their land. Some soldiers did not want to move, but they sold their bounties to people who did. Old newspapers record the land sales as people moved farther and farther west. Settlers hopscotched from Virginia to Kentucky to Missouri or from Ohio to Indiana to Illinois. A great example of how this worked is seen in *The Little House on the Prairie* books of Laura Ingalls Wilder. These books tell the story

Settlers moved westward during the early part of the nineteenth century. Some reached the Blue Ridge Mountains in Kentucky *(right)*.

of Wilder's own childhood. The fictional family moves from Wisconsin to Minnesota, then to Kansas, and eventually to the Dakota Territory (North Dakota and South Dakota).

Louisiana Purchase

The move westward exploded with the Louisiana Purchase. In 1803 President Thomas Jefferson bought more than 525 million acres of land from France. The land included everything from the Appalachian Mountains to the Rocky Mountains. From this land came all or part of fourteen states. These are Arkansas, Missouri, Iowa, Minnesota, North Dakota, South Dakota, Nebraska, New Mexico, Texas, Oklahoma, Kansas, Montana, Wyoming, and, of course, Louisiana. The Louisiana Purchase doubled the size of the

In this image, Thomas Jefferson *(left)* signs the Louisiana Purchase Treaty in 1803. It doubled the size of the United States. In reality, Jefferson did not sign the treaty. Three diplomats signed it, and the U.S. Senate ratified it later that year.

United States. It opened vast territories for the expanding U.S. population. All that territory also gave the United States the resources needed to become an international power.

As the Louisiana Purchase moved U.S. borders farther west, south, and north, it created tension with other countries. One of the countries that felt threatened was Spain. The northern border of New Spain, a Spanish colony, met the southern border of the United States. New Spain included all of modern-day Mexico and all of Texas, New Mexico, Arizona, California, Nevada, Utah, Colorado, Wyoming, and Florida.

The Louisiana Purchase also revived the issue of slavery. The northern and southern parts of the United States disagreed about slavery. Most northerners wanted to prevent slavery from spreading into any new territory that the United States acquired. Southerners wanted to be able to take their slaves with them when they settled in the new lands.

Although a good deal of debate took place in the U.S. Congress, the treaty with France to purchase the land was finally ratified in late October 1803. Jefferson sent Captain Meriwether Lewis and Lieutenant William Clark to lead a team to travel to the far reaches of the new land and beyond. Their job was to report back to the president everything and everyone they found—the peoples, the geography, and the plant and animal life. The information they collected fueled U.S. interest in settling this new western territory. As expected, people immediately began moving into it.

Lewis and Clark explored the Louisiana Territory for Thomas Jefferson. Along the way, they encountered many Native American tribes, some helpful and some warlike. This illustration is from 1811. It was printed to illustrate a journal by a member of the Lewis and Clark party.

NEW SPAIN

The Spanish government had claimed the land that later became Texas in 1519, long before any English settlements were in the Americas. The Spanish explorer Francisco Vazquez de Coronado led a team to map out the territory of New Spain in 1541. He found a vast territory rich in minerals. It was occupied by native peoples, some with a high degree of civilization. The Aztec civilization, conquered by the Spanish conquistadors, was known for its skilled engineers, mathematicians, and astronomers. The Aztecs had a sophisticated and complex culture, and they left behind impressive art that can still be seen.

By 1685 the French had also begun to explore the same territory, sailing down the Mississippi River from their

This painting by Frederick Remington shows Coronado *(center on white horse)* crossing the plains of what later became Kansas. A Native American *(second from left)* guides Coronado and his team through the uncharted lands.

colony, New France (Canada). Spain decided it needed to settle the northern areas of New Spain so France couldn't claim them. The Spanish government first sent in Franciscan priests to bring the Roman Catholic faith to the native peoples.

In 1718 the Franciscans built a mission church in the area they called San Antonio de Bexar. The Spanish government built a fort nearby for protection. Over the years, the place was known as Bejar, Bexar, San Antonio, or by its nickname, the Alamo. The nickname came from the Spanish word for the cottonwood trees growing near-by. The first official civilian settlement in Texas came in 1731. Fifteen families from the Spanish Canary Islands settled at San Antonio.

An American named Moses Austin took advantage of New Spain's desire to settle the province of Texas. He petitioned the Spanish government to become an *empresario*. Empresarios received grants of land for two hundred or

This statue of Moses Austin stands in modern San Antonio, Texas. Austin first petitioned the Spanish government to bring Anglos (white settlers) into Texas.

more families. They then recruited the families and settled them on the land. The empresario was in charge of his little colony. Each family that migrated paid a fee to Austin for the land.

MOSES AND STEPHEN AUSTIN

Moses Austin requested a grant of land for three hundred families. The provincial governor, Antonio Martínez, accepted his request and forwarded it on to Mexico City, the capital of New Spain. He advised the government to accept "the proposal he is making . . . which is bound to provide for the increase and prosperity of this province." The central government approved the grant, and Moses Austin

Stephen Austin *(right)* continued the plans his father, Moses, had set in motion. Stephen presided over the settlement of the Texas lands his father had been granted by the Spanish government.

returned home to recruit the families. He died shortly after returning to the United States, however.

Meanwhile, New Spain gained independence from Spain in 1821. It became the Republic of Mexico in 1824. As a result, Moses' son, Stephen, took over the grant. He led a group of about three hundred families to settle in Texas. Later, writing to a friend, Austin told him that Texas "will be the best, the brightest star in the Mexican constellation." He would do the work to make it so.

Austin was generous in his terms to his settlers. Each family received a grant of 320 acres of farmland along a river and 640 acres of grazing land farther inland. The head of the family could claim additional land in the names of his wife and children and also 50 additional acres for each slave he owned. The settlers paid Austin a fee of twelve and a half cents for each acre granted to them within three years of receiving their land. Austin accepted payment in "any kind of property that will not be a dead loss to me, such as

"[Austin's] proposal . . . is bound to provide for the increase and prosperity of this province."

—Antonio Martínez, 1820

horses, mules, cattle, hogs, peltry, furs, bees wax, home made cloth, dressed deer-skins, etc."

A mixed group of white settlers came from the United States to Texas, and they came for many reasons. Some were looking for a fresh financial start. Others wanted to leave personal problems, such as unhappy marriages, behind them. Here, as in most of the U.S. frontier, settlers saw a chance for adventure. Many came just because the territory was unknown, and they could be part of civilizing it.

The U.S. settlers coming into the territory had to accept the terms of the Mexican constitution of 1824. This constitution included the requirements given to Moses Austin in his original grant. Settlers had to meet the "first and principal requisite of being Catholics . . . taking the necessary oath, to be obedient in all things to the government, to take up arms in its defence against all kinds of enemies." The settlers freely agreed to this constitution and accepted the

Settlers, like this family, moved to Texas to farm or raise livestock.

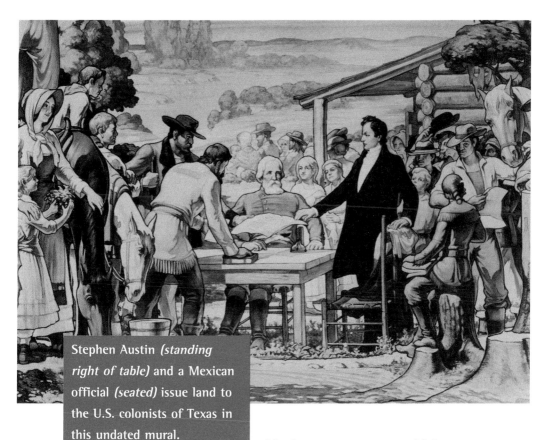

Stephen Austin *(standing right of table)* and a Mexican official *(seated)* issue land to the U.S. colonists of Texas in this undated mural.

Mexican government, which promised "that they should continue to enjoy that constitutional liberty and republican government to which they had been habituated in the land of their birth, the United States of America."

Austin was a successful empresario, and his colony thrived. The difficulties in the early years were mostly local disputes. Especially aggravating to Austin were the people who complained that he was making a profit by acting as empresario. He wrote to a friend in 1826 that his colonists "say that I ought to do everything for them free, because the government has already paid me in the lands that came to me as empresario . . . but I cannot eat them [the lands], make clothes of them, nor sell them." Even so, both Austin and his

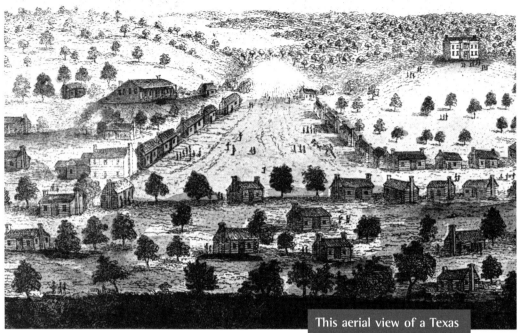

This aerial view of a Texas settlement in the early nineteenth century shows how the Anglo population exploded in Texas.

colonists must have benefited from the arrangement, since Austin later petitioned and received more land for other families.

The population of the area exploded from about seven thousand Anglos around 1800 to around thirty thousand by the early 1830s. Almost all the growth in population was from American immigration. In 1830 the Mexican government became alarmed at the numbers of Americans settling in Texas. It passed a new law that prohibited any more immigration from the United States.

A military leader, General Antonio López de Santa Anna, took advantage of Mexican fears about the growing American numbers. He got himself elected president of Mexico in 1833. Santa Anna quickly declared an emergency and ruled as a dictator. He vowed to bring all the Mexican provinces, including Texas, under strong central control.

STATISTICS ON THE TEXAS SETTLEMENT

Population of Mexico, 1830	6,000,000
Population of province of Texas, 1835	about 53,000
Anglos	30,000
slaves	5,000
Mexicans	3,470
native peoples	14,200

He also vowed to relocate people he viewed as trouble makers to land farther from the U.S. border.

Rebellions erupted throughout Mexico as provincial governments fought to maintain local control. The residents of Texas watched with concern as each rebellion was crushed. They prepared to confront Santa Anna themselves. Their defiance earned them special attention from the dictator.

> **" . . . as to the future . . . it is a prospect of confusion, disorder, and civil war."**
>
> —Stephen F. Austin, 1835

CHAPTER TWO

THE ROAD TO WAR

Both sides in the Texas Revolution claimed they were acting nobly and with the best interests of all at heart. However, both the Texians and Santa Anna's Mexican government had other, differing agendas that weren't nearly so noble.

TEXAS DIVIDED

Historians estimate that the Texians could be divided into three groups. The first small faction was a peace party. Stephen Austin was part of that group at first. These people believed that the differences with the Mexican government could be worked out. The second small faction was made up of "those who believed that Texas could no longer hope for anything save injustice and oppression from the Mexican government." They wanted independence. Most of the citizenry made up the third group. They were quite content to remain neutral and avoid the wrath of the Mexican government.

The Texians who wanted independence used the ideas of the American Revolution to defend their position. They said the Mexican government was guilty of "denial of religious toleration and the restrictions on slavery... the prohibition of immigration from the United States." They were correct. The situation in Mexico had changed since they had agreed to their terms of settlement, resulting in "the cruel alternatives either to abandon our homes... or submit to... the combined despotism of the sword and the priest-

> ## "[T]he cruel alternatives [were] either to abandon our homes... or submit to... the combined despotism of the sword and the priesthood."
> —Texas Declaration of Independence, 1836

hood," as the Texas Declaration of Independence later stated. When they settled in Texas, the settlers had a great deal of political freedom. They mostly governed themselves locally. Santa Anna wanted a strong centralized government under his personal control. That meant that the Texians and the people in the other provinces—who were just as angry at the changes under Santa Anna—lost freedoms that they'd had before he rose to power.

THE SLAVERY ISSUE

The Texians helped create the conflict too. Many Texians were slaveholders. Many were actively trying to start a revolution. They thought that if Texas became independent, the Texas territories could be admitted to the United States as slave states. In fact, many in the United States saw this revolution as a "criminal land grab... a Southern attempt to spread slavocracy." One news account referred

Slaves work on a cotton plantation in the early nineteenth century. Many Texians owned slaves, including Alamo commander William Barret Travis.

to "the dark forces of slave-holding tyranny, . . . fraud and corruption, by which the . . . annexation of Texas [was] to be effected."

Slavery was becoming a very heated topic in the United States. The Texas issue provided ammunition for both sides of the national debate. Ironically, the actions of Santa Anna in centralizing control of Texas as a Mexican state changed the subject of that debate. After the Alamo, history didn't see Texas statehood as a slavery issue but remembered only the gallant stand of the Alamo defenders.

THE NEED TO DISCIPLINE THE TEXIANS

Mexican president Santa Anna brought his own mix of motives. He was right in thinking that many Texians wanted independence no matter what he chose to do. He disagreed with Mexico's original decisions to grant land to Americans. In his autobiography, he wrote that the earlier government acted "with an unbelievable lack of discretion" in granting land to the Texian colonists. He was determined to correct that mistake.

Santa Anna, in his own statements, called the Texians "pirates and outlaws." He said he was "determined to carry on a war of extermination." He called the Texians "perfidious wretches" and referred to them as serpents who stung the person who had saved them.

Santa Anna's determination to drive out or relocate the Texians, combined with the Texians' determination to defend their rights, could only end in bloodshed. Stephen Austin tried to be the peacemaker among the Texian leaders. He visited Mexico City in 1833 to try to negotiate with the government. He requested autonomy for Texas within a Mexican government. Instead, he was imprisoned for eighteen months. No one knows for sure who ordered his arrest, although most assume it was Santa Anna. Austin was never charged with a crime during his imprisonment. He was not allowed to plead his case for release before any court. He was simply transferred from prison to prison and then finally released. His experiences in prison changed him into a supporter of independence.

In April 1835, Austin wrote a letter that proved to be very prophetic. He wrote: "I am still here [as a] prisoner....No one I believe pretends to make any

> "I am still here [as a] prisoner. . . . No one I believe pretends to make any certain calculations as to the future—except that it is a prospect of confusion, disorder, and civil war."
>
> —Stephen Austin, 1835

certain calculations as to the future—except that it is a prospect of confusion, disorder, and civil war."

One other event occurred that might have changed the outcome of the struggle. The U.S. government made offers to buy Texas from Mexico. The Mexican government turned them down. Santa Anna viewed them as an insult. The offers only fueled his belief that the United States was trying to take Texas from Mexico.

By 1835 Santa Anna was dealing with at least eight separate open rebellions in Mexico. His solutions were military and brutal as he suppressed each rebellion in turn. One historian noted that the Texians should have heeded Santa Anna's actions in May 1835 in Zacatecas. There, he had killed the rebels and then allowed his victorious army to rampage through the area for a full two days. Santa Anna punished not only active resisters but the innocent caught in his path.

THE TEXIANS DECLARE WAR

Watching the situation as it developed in the rest of Mexico, the Texians decided that it was time to act. In October 1835, the colonists formed a committee headed by Stephen Austin. It was charged with guaranteeing the safety of the colony from aggression by the central government under Santa Anna. A Mexican army, led by Santa Anna's brother-in-law, General Martín Perfecto de Cos, arrived in the territory to fortify the Alamo at San Antonio. Austin called for the local militias to form a Texian army to resist. Cos responded with an attempt to capture the Texians and disarm them. He established himself at the Alamo on October 9, 1835. The Texians seized and fortified the fort at Goliad.

Only a small spark was needed to begin a war. The spark came when Mexican authorities notified the Texas town of Gonzales that they were confiscating its small cannon. The town resisted the demands and called for help from their fellow Texians. As tensions rose, a Texian army of four hundred men, led by Austin, attacked General Cos's troops on October 28, 1835. The Battle of Concepción was fought along the San Antonio River. Even though they were outnumbered, the Texians defeated the Mexicans, causing heavy casualties among the soldados.

Knowing that they were facing a serious conflict with the Mexican army, the Texians appointed Sam Houston as commander in chief of their army. He called for five thousand men to serve until the

Sam Houston was appointed the commander in chief of the Texian army in 1835.

General Cos was the Mexican commander who surrendered the Alamo to the Texians in December 1835.

conflict ended. The Mexican and Texian armies met again in late November, and the Texians killed more than fifty Mexican soldiers. The Texians lost only two. The campaign climaxed on December 5, when a group of three hundred volunteers began a siege of the Mexicans at the Alamo fort. On December 9, General Cos surrendered the fort to the Texians. He then returned to Mexico City to report his defeat to Santa Anna. The Texian army was sent home for the winter, leaving only a few troops to man the garrison forts.

Santa Anna was furious about the defeat of Cos. He immediately began preparing his own troops for the long march to Texas. He was determined to finish the war in Texas and remove from Mexican soil the Anglos, whom he saw as traitors to Mexico. Houston called on Texians to resist the coming invasion by an enemy who "has sworn to extinguish us, or sweep us from the sod."

Stephen Austin had moved from pacifist to ardent supporter of independence. He wrote to Houston on January 7, 1836, "I wish to see Texas free from the trammels of religious intolerance and other anti-republican restrictions, and independent at once; and as an individual have always been ready to risk my all to obtain it." Both sides were ready to move decisively.

> **"** [W]e will rather die in these ditches than give up to the enemy."
>
> —Jim Bowie, February 2, 1836

THE
CHAPTER THREE
PERSONALITIES

Among the defenders of the Alamo were a few men whose personalities determined the events that took place in February and March of 1836. Any one of several people had the power to change that outcome. Each of them, for various reasons, allowed the battle to occur. They did so either by active decisions or passive failure to respond to the decisions of others. To understand the Alamo, one has to know more about William Barret Travis, Jim Bowie, David Crockett, James Fannin, Sam Houston, and Antonio López de Santa Anna. All of them held the future in their hands in February 1836. All of them brought to the Alamo their own stories, which shaped their choices there.

WILLIAM BARRET TRAVIS, UNLUCKY COMMANDER

William Barret Travis, the military commander at the Alamo, was not supposed to be in command when the siege began on February 23,

William Barret Travis became commander of the Alamo garrison by accident, when the original commander, James Neill, was called away.

1836. Born in South Carolina, he was a descendant of the original settlers at Jamestown, Virginia. He was only twenty-six years old when he arrived at the Alamo, but he had already lived a full and interesting life. After spending his earliest years in South Carolina, his family relocated to Alabama. There he began a career as a schoolteacher while reading law with a local attorney. By the age of twenty, he was married and practicing law. But he was still restless. Two years later, he was a father, the editor of a newspaper he had begun, and an officer in the Alabama militia. Accused of murder, he fled to Texas, leaving his estranged wife behind.

Travis took to his new life in Texas, practicing law and becoming involved with the group of people who advocated Texas independence. His wife finally divorced him in 1835 and sent their child, Charles Edward Travis, to live with his father in Texas. In January 1836, Travis was commissioned a lieutenant colonel in the new Texas army and told to recruit men to fight with him. Travis was ordered to take his new recruits to James Neill, the garrison commander at the

Alamo. When Neill left the Alamo because of family problems, Travis found himself in charge.

Travis is remembered most for his moving letters begging for assistance to shore up the defenders of the fort. Although the letters are widely quoted, very few actually date from the time of the Alamo siege. On February 23, Travis wrote a short note to James Fannin at Goliad, requesting that he come to reinforce the Alamo. The next day, he wrote perhaps his most famous letter, addressed "To the people of Texas and All Americans in the World." It is the source of his often quoted pledge to never surrender. His next letter is to

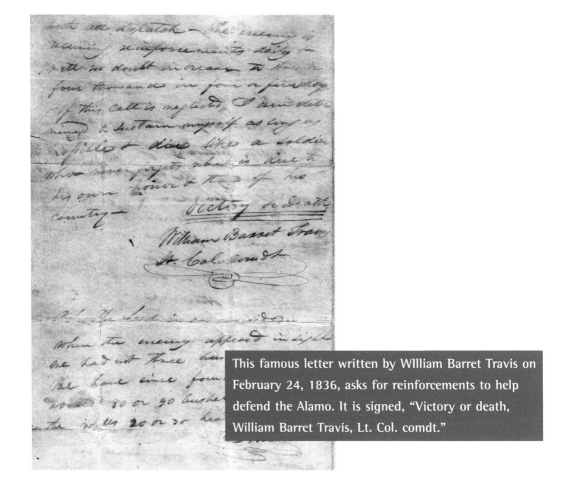

This famous letter written by WIlliam Barret Travis on February 24, 1836, asks for reinforcements to help defend the Alamo. It is signed, "Victory or death, William Barret Travis, Lt. Col. comdt."

his commander in chief, Sam Houston, and is not really a letter. It is a report dated February 25 on the military actions taken so far. He wrote another report on activities on March 3, this time addressed to the president of the convention that was meeting to discuss possible independence. This letter is often cited for his remarks on the "blood red banner" flying over the Mexican lines. The same day, he wrote two personal letters, one to a friend, speaking about his dream of Texas independence. The other was his final letter to his son's guardian, in which Travis asked that six-year-old Charles be raised with "the proud recollection that he is the son of a man who died for his country." Travis is remembered for the eloquence of these letters. Unfortunately, Travis's skill with words was not matched with equal military or leadership skills.

His principal biographer described him as lacking "a charismatic personality." Another called him a "head-strong, high-stepping, opportunistic fellow." David Crockett called him gallant and said that Travis would make Santa Anna "have snakes to eat before he gets over the wall, I tell you." In truth, Travis was faced with the nearly impossible task of taking a group of very independent and strong-willed citizen soldiers and trying to form them into an effective army. It did not help that his co-commander was Jim Bowie. Bowie was a better and more experienced military leader. He undermined and criticized every action Travis took as Travis attempted to ready the garrison for battle. As commander, Travis also had the authority to abandon the fort if he felt that it could not be successfully defended.

Travis cared passionately about the cause of Texas independence. As a slaveholder, independence would have been good for him economically. But he also believed that Texas was destined to join the United States.

Jim Bowie, Adventurer

Jim Bowie had a long and interesting history before ending up at the Alamo. Born in Kentucky, he was a land speculator, a gambler, and a treasure hunter. He had migrated along the frontier from Kentucky to Tennessee, on to Missouri, and then to Louisiana before ending up in Texas. He even found a long-lost gold and silver mine in Texas. His family were slaveholders. *The Handbook of Texas*, a database on Texas history, describes him as "well traveled, convivial . . . generous . . . ambitious and scheming; he played cards for money, and lived in a world of debt." More important, for the defenders of the Alamo, he had taken part in a number of military expeditions and was a good commander. He already knew William Travis. Travis was his attorney and had drafted some legal documents for him on land transactions.

Although Jim Bowie *(left)* was not formally an officer in the Texian army, he was given joint command at the Alamo.

THE BOWIE KNIFE

Alamo defender Jim Bowie is perhaps more famous for the knife that bears his name than for his death at the Alamo. His brother Resin Bowie actually created the Bowie knife. The knife Resin made for his brother around 1827 is thought to have had a blade about nine inches long and over an inch wide. Unlike other knives of the time, the upper edge of the blade was also sharpened. It was Jim Bowie, however, who made the knife famous. In a duel in Mississippi known as the Sandbar Fight, he used his new knife to disembowel a man who had attacked him.

The legend continues that Jim Bowie thought this knife was actually too small. He had a larger one crafted for him—over a foot long and three inches wide. Bowie was known as a skilled knife fighter, and according to David Crockett, he had his knife with him at the Alamo. After that, Bowie's knife disappeared, and no one really knows what it actually looked like. Everyone in the West seemed to want one though. Several blacksmiths claimed they had made knives for Jim Bowie, and they did a booming business selling blades that were similar to his.

Bowie was sent by Houston, commander in chief of the Texian forces, to determine what should be done with the fortress at the Alamo. Houston wanted to have the old mission fort torn down and the militia moved to a more defensible position. Bowie, along with about thirty of his troops, arrived at the Alamo in January. On February 2, 1836, Bowie sent a letter to the provisional governor of Texas, Henry Smith. In it he recommended that the fort should be held. "The salvation of Texas," he wrote, "depends on keeping [the Alamo] out of the hands of the enemy. . . . [W]e will rather die in these ditches than give up to the enemy. The citizens deserve our patriotism, and the public safety demands our lives rather than evacuate this post to the enemy."

> "The citizens deserve our patriotism, and the public safety demands our lives rather than evacuate this post to the enemy."
>
> —Jim Bowie, February 2, 1836

Bowie and Travis were co-commanders of the garrison after James Neill left. The men had very different ideas on how to train the garrison and prepare the fort for an attack. The shared command did not last, but not because of their differences of opinion. Bowie became extremely ill, and Travis took over full command.

DAVID CROCKETT, FRONTIERSMAN AND STORYTELLER

Many of the Alamo defenders became famous after the fight for Texas independence. Only one of the defenders walked into the Alamo as a legend.

David—and it was David, not Davy as he is known in modern times—had captured public imagination as a frontiersman, sharpshooter, storyteller, author, and an outspoken congressman from Tennessee. Defeated for reelection to Congress, he decided to explore the new frontier in Texas. He thought he might move his family there. As he left office, he said, "You may all go to hell and I will go to Texas." Unlike many of the other Alamo defenders, he had not been part of the push for Texas independence. Once there, however, he found the kind of fight he liked to join. One biographer wrote of him—and of the Tennessee Mounted Volunteers who came with him to the Alamo—that all of them were proud of being descendants of soldiers who had fought in the American Revolution. He noted, they "practiced high-mindedness with a passion." It was a good characterization of Crockett and his

David Crockett, shown here in a formal set-
ting in 1820, spent seven years in the U.S.
House of Representatives for Tennessee. He
is the most famous of the Alamo defenders.

friends. All were proud of
their heritage. They saw
their role as preserving the
spirit of their ancestors by involving themselves in the cause of liberty.

No one knows why Crockett did not intervene in the quarrels
between Travis and Bowie. Nor do we know why he did not try to
influence the decisions being made by them. Crockett brought to
the Alamo unquestioned bravery and integrity. He was the one person with the moral authority to force a decision to withdraw from
the Alamo. He could have encouraged the Texians to fight another
day from a more advantageous position. But he chose not to do so.

JAMES WALKER FANNIN JR., INDECISIVE RESCUER

Houston believed that James Fannin should have saved the
Alamo. Fannin, who had studied at the military academy at West
Point, had more military knowledge than most of the Texians. But
he was indecisive.

James Walker Fannin Jr. *(left)* was in charge of the fort at Goliad at the time of the siege of the Alamo. Although Travis requested his help, Fannin never arrived with reinforcements.

Fannin was in command of more than four hundred men at the fort at Goliad. He actually started out toward the Alamo once word of the siege arrived. Shortly into the march, however, a wagon broke down. Fannin, already having second thoughts about leaving the safety of Goliad, decided to turn back. If Fannin had arrived at the Alamo, he would have tripled the number of defenders. They might have been able to withstand Santa Anna's assault. Fannin's decision to turn back sealed the fate of the Alamo defenders.

SAMUEL HOUSTON, FATHER OF TEXAS

Sam Houston was a complex man. In the War of 1812, he joined the army and fought under the command of Andrew Jackson, who became his mentor and friend. After leaving the army, he became a lawyer and then was elected to Congress. Eventually, as governor of

Tennessee, he gained knowledge of the law and government. After a failed marriage, he abandoned his political career and disappeared into the wilderness to live with the Cherokee for three years. He acquired an understanding of the needs of the native peoples that was unusual at the time. Several years later, returning to public life in Washington, D.C., he lost his temper with a political opponent. He assaulted the man with a cane and was arrested. After being reprimanded and forced to pay a fine, he gave up U.S. politics and went to Texas in 1832 to make a fresh start.

No sooner had he arrived than he became part of the growing independence movement. All the experiences of his life had prepared him for his role there. As commander in chief of the Texian troops, Houston was charged with protecting the volunteers at the Alamo. He sent his friend Jim Bowie to assess the military readiness of the fort. However, Houston then accepted Bowie's response that the fort must be defended, in spite of his own belief that the Alamo was "a trap for anyone who dared to defend it."

While the siege at the Alamo was taking place, Houston was negotiating with local native tribes for their support. He also attended the convention of Texians that declared Texas independence. Some historians feel that he deliberately allowed the siege to take place. It gave him the incident he needed to unite the wavering settlers of Texas in support of independence. Those who hadn't wanted to get involved were sure to change their minds after a brutal Mexican attack.

ANTONIO LÓPEZ DE SANTA ANNA, NAPOLEON OF THE WEST

Santa Anna's two nicknames, Don Demonio (Sir Demon or Devil) and the Napoleon of the West, say much about his personality. He was involved in the rebellion that achieved Mexico's independence from Spain. He went on to be the president of Mexico no fewer than eleven times in twenty

Antonio López de Santa Anna *(left)* joined the army at the age of sixteen. He fought in the Mexican war for independence from Spain and was involved in the early days of the republic. He was elected president for the first time in 1833.

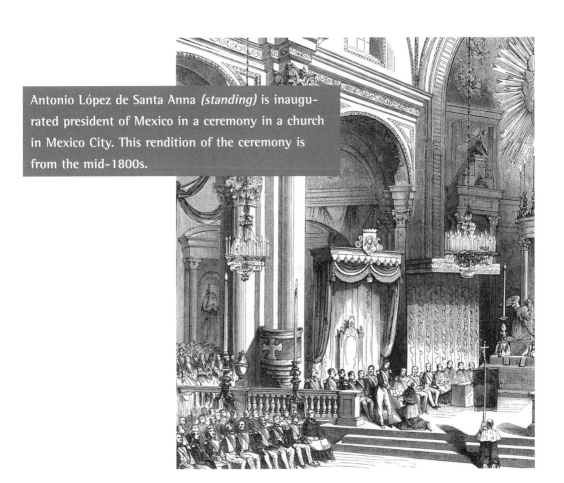

Antonio López de Santa Anna *(standing)* is inaugurated president of Mexico in a ceremony in a church in Mexico City. This rendition of the ceremony is from the mid–1800s.

years. His actions as president always led to his overthrow within a short time. Then he would return to power when the needs of the country could not be met by other leaders. Time after time, he rescued his country and then alienated its citizens by his actions.

His autobiography reveals a man convinced that he was the only one who knew what was right for Mexico. His writings equally show he felt that any disagreement with him was evidence of conspiracy and treason. He wrote of himself as "zealous in the fulfillment of my duties to my country" and "dominated by a noble ambition." Santa Anna blamed failures on others. He spoke of one enemy's "perfidy" and "scandalous acts" in opposing him. When a general did not

Of Coonskin Caps and Recycling

The people living on the frontier were, by necessity, recyclers. They had no department stores or sporting goods stores to shop at. Many of those on the frontier would never have had access to more than a small general store. These settlers were used to killing the meat that their families ate. Like the Native Americans who lived nearby, they did not waste any part of their kill. Anyone who did did not survive for long.

The skins of the raccoons that were trapped were used to make warm coonskin hats with the tails left on. The deer they killed for meat were skinned. The leather from the tanned skin was used to make clothing that was both rugged and waterproof. Skins were also used for shoes and blankets and for door and window coverings to keep out the cold. Shirts and undergarments were made from homespun cotton or linen made from flax plants. Their entire wardrobe might include only things that came from nature.

Some may be amused by the strange garb of the frontier people. They, however, would probably be shocked at the size of modern closets and the amount of clothing in them.

---

simply adventurers who saw this as an opportunity to serve Texas and then be rewarded with land in the area. Very few of the defenders actually came from the area around San Antonio. Local defenders responded in case of an attack.

In fact, the Alamo defenders were a hodgepodge of people. Some brought real military skill to the Alamo. Others brought simply the normal level of military ability expected of all males of the time. Each man found himself in the Alamo for his own personal reasons. But each of them was "seeking a successful life, not a glorious death."

Because of the lack of good records from the time, historians give varying estimates of the number of defenders at the Alamo. The experts also disagree on why the defenders were there and their skill level as fighters. However, historians do agree on some points. The defenders came from eighteen states in the United States. They were not primarily trained soldiers. They represented the usual run of occupations found in most small communities of the time. There were lots of farmers, of course. But all the other professionals that made up a frontier settlement—doctors, lawyers, blacksmiths, brick masons, and preachers—were also in the mix. They represented a wide range of ages, from perhaps fifteen to mid-fifties.

As citizen soldiers, most did not wear uniforms. Some of those who made up the resident garrison under Travis's command, however, had managed to become uniformed. The Texian army was just getting organized, so exact numbers are impossible to find. They did not have the supplies of a more traditional army, though. Crockett's and Bowie's men brought their own supplies. The military leaders of the garrison, noted Texas historian Ben Proctor, "had no money to buy military stores or pay the soldiers, no food or clothing . . . no adequate number of horses either for scout or for transportation."

Travis tried to organize this group into some semblance of an army. He made them drill and do military exercises that would develop their ability to fight as a unit. But the men did not take well to his demands and training. These were independent people whose lives depended on their own fighting skills. They saw no need for drill in battle techniques or military exercises to make them fight more effectively.

TRYING TO TRAIN THE ALAMO DEFENDERS

Lieutenant Colonel William Barret Travis faced an impossible task in attempting to train the Alamo defenders to fight as a cohesive military force. These men felt they had developed the skills they needed to protect the Alamo in their everyday lives.

Living on the frontier did require a great deal of skill with weapons. Pioneer families lived in isolation from their nearest neighbors. All members of the family had to be able to defend themselves *(below)*. Men had the additional training in weapons that came from hunting to supply the family with food and clothing. They also needed to be able to defend their families from local native peoples. Frontier people were skilled with their rifles, knives, and tomahawks.

A modern soldier usually has to be taught how to fight and how to use weapons. These are not skills that most recruits learned as a child, the way the Alamo defenders had. Thus, the basic training was already in place before these men ever arrived at the Alamo. The negative side of all this independence is that each defender felt he could handle the Mexican attackers. As a result, the group never was a cohesive fighting unit.

They felt quite capable of handling the situation without any training the military could offer. "The men," noted one historian, "did as they pleased, sometimes refusing either to drill or go on patrol."

TEJANO ALLIES

Fighting alongside the Texians were two other groups, often forgotten in stories of the Alamo. The first group was the Tejanos, Mexicans who lived in the area prior to Anglo settlement. Historians estimate that about thirty-five hundred indigenous Mexicans along with about thirty-five thousand Anglos lived in the province at the time of the revolution. Many of these Tejanos felt as strongly as the Anglos that they could not tolerate the tyrannical rule of Santa Anna. Best known of the Tejanos is Captain Juan Seguín. Seguín was the courier Travis sent to Colonel Fannin at Goliad to try to convince

Tejanos, people of Spanish or Mexican descent who lived in Texas prior to the Anglo settlement, lived on large ranches throughout the Texas territory.

Juan Seguín was born into a prominent Tejano family. Both he and his father served in politics during their lives.

him to reinforce the Alamo defenders. Seguín was involved in the fight against Santa Anna from its beginning in October 1835. Another Tejano, Francisco Ruiz, the *alcalde* (mayor) of San Antonio, provided the best eyewitness account of the actual attack on the Alamo from his place in town.

The second group supporting the defenders of the Alamo were the slaves owned by some of the men. At that time, about one-seventh of the population of Texas were slaves. Many of the landowners who had the most interest in securing Texas's independence were slaveholders. So it is not surprising that some of the defenders of the Alamo were slaves who had accompanied their owners. The most famous was Travis's slave, Joe (for whom no last name is known). Twenty-three-year-old Joe later said that several slaves were at the Alamo, giving historians their only source of information on who might have been there.

SEASONAL WARFARE

In earlier times, land wars were fought only in certain seasons. The transport of men and supplies was just about impossible in winter and during the spring rains. The defenders of the Alamo were caught by surprise when General Santa Anna and his soldados arrived in February. The idea of moving an army of six to eight thousand men and their equipment across the plains in winter was unheard of. Only an extremely motivated and disciplined commander, like Santa Anna, would undertake such a journey.

Before the days of railroad travel, the military had only two real modes of transportation. The best one was by water. Boats could transport men and materials easily. If the area could not be reached by water, troops had to march overland. Supplies for the soldiers were carried in carts pulled by oxen. Winter is the rainy season in Texas, and the ground turns muddy. A general would not normally choose to move cannons on oxcarts through the winter mud.

Santa Anna gathered his army in Monclova, Mexico, about six hundred miles from San Antonio. From there they began their forced march to the Alamo in the rain and cold. His soldiers were not equipped with proper clothing and shoes. A large number of the men died or deserted along the way.

THE SOLDADOS OF MEXICO

Santa Anna managed to move a force of more than six thousand men across Mexico in winter—a military accomplishment of which he could rightly be proud. His soldados included some trained soldiers as well as new recruits. Historian Jeff Long writes that the recruits were "illiterate, impoverished, and superstitious." They were, he also noted, "cannon fodder." Poorly outfitted in ill-fitting, lightweight clothing and shoes, they suffered greatly on the forced march to the Alamo.

The Alamo defenders had expected that Santa Anna could not possibly arrive from Mexico City until at least March 15. The army arrived on February 22, which illustrates the pace at which it was forced to move. The fast pace cost Santa Anna dearly in the lives of soldiers and the animals used to transport their supplies. Santa Anna's autobiography speaks of the hardships of winter travel. He wrote of the need to use plants and wild animals for rations and the difficulty crossing rivers for the soldiers and the oxcarts. He said his army was deserving of "the gratitude of the nation."

On the day before the battle, Santa Anna issued a general order detailing his plan of attack. In it he called on "each man to fulfill his duties and to exert himself to give his country a day of glory and satisfaction." Some historians noted that he gave another order to the officers, "to cut down any of their comrades who falter or retreat." General Santa Anna was determined that his fighters would be victorious in the coming battle.

> **"[A] blood-red banner waves from the church of Bejar, and in the camp above us, in token that the war is one of vengeance."**
>
> —William Barret Travis, March 3, 1836

CHAPTER FIVE

THE SIEGE

"This man [Santa Anna] was every inch a leader," remembered Enrique Esparza. Esparza was only eight years old when he saw Santa Anna and his army arrive to begin the siege of the Alamo. As the Texian garrison moved to their fortress, the townspeople became eyewitnesses to the thirteen-day siege that began on February 23, 1836.

THE SIEGE BEGINS

The defenders of the fort also watched his arrival with great interest. "Early this morning, the enemy came in sight, marching in regular order, and displaying their strength to the greatest advantage, in order to strike us with terror," wrote David Crockett in his diary. The strategy did not work, added Crockett. "That was no go; they will find that they have to do with men who will never lay down their arms as long as they can stand on their legs."

> "Early this morning, the enemy came in sight, marching in regular order, and displaying their strength to the greatest advantage, in order to strike us with terror."
>
> —David Crocket, 1836

Crockett's journal was found after the battle. It was published two years later with a chapter added that detailed what had happened after his entries ended on March 5. The diary is the best source of information for what was happening in the Alamo during the thirteen days that the siege lasted. Some of it

The Alamo, 1836

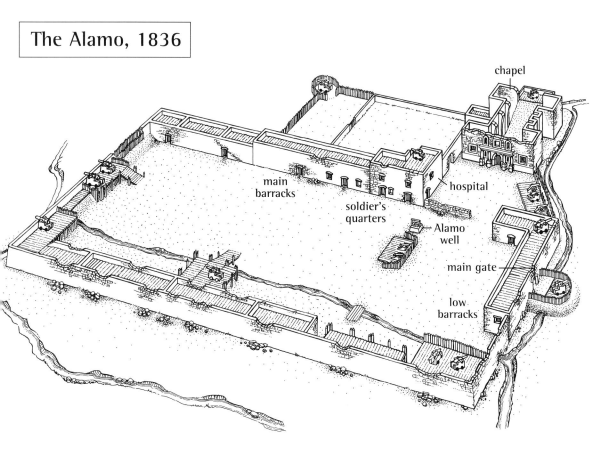

chapel

main barracks

hospital

soldier's quarters

Alamo well

main gate

low barracks

is humorous. Crockett describes an ineffective artillery attack by Santa Anna's troops as "not unlike a pitched battle in the Hall of Congress, where the parties array their forces . . . then fire away with loud sounding speeches." The tone rapidly turns serious in the same entry, however, when he mentions that "provisions are becoming scarce, and the enemy are endeavouring to cut off our water."

> "Provisions are becoming scarce, and the enemy are endeavouring to cut off our water."
>
> **—David Crockett, 1836**

Santa Anna arrived with forces that so outnumbered the defenders that he could have captured the fort the same day. The defenders were taken by surprise, and most were living in the nearby town when the Mexicans arrived. The accommodations in town were much more comfortable than those in the fort. Most of the defenders had chosen to be comfortable while they could. "The Texans lounging in town barely had time to grab a few provisions and fall back into the Alamo," wrote historian James Crisp. They were able to retrieve supplies in the days ahead, since the siege was a loose one.

Messengers regularly traveled in and out of the lines. Travis was able to send out a messenger to deliver a letter to Colonel Fannin at Goliad. One defender left the fort and escaped during the siege. The siege was tight enough, of course, so that all the defenders could not have marched away. If Fannin and his men had tried to relieve the siege, they would have had to fight their way in. However, not counting major movements of men or supplies from outside, the siege did allow for some movement between the town and the fort.

WORSENING CONDITIONS

Even so, food began to run low inside the fort. One of the defenders, Isaac Millsaps, wrote to his wife on March 3, telling her that they had "beef and corn to eat but no coffee." He was hoping for help to arrive, as were all the defenders. Travis's pleas for reinforcements led everyone to believe that fresh troops and supplies were on their way.

Santa Anna was worried that the defenders might be reinforced if he waited to attack. But, he also knew that his own troops needed time to rest. Or perhaps the delay in attacking was a psychological trick he played on the defenders. Citing Santa Anna's report, historian Richard Santos indicated that on the first day of the siege, after examining the defenses of the Alamo, Santa Anna "returned to headquarters and ordered the band 'to entertain the Texans with selected music and periodic artillery barrages.'"

Other historians noted that San Antonio de Bexar and the Alamo were much too small to be barriers to Santa Anna's progress through Texas. He could have easily left a small portion of his army to guard the Alamo and then bypassed the area. Many historians agree that he did not do so because he was seeking revenge for the earlier Texian conquest of the fort.

THE BLOOD-RED BANNER

The defenders were aware that revenge was Santa Anna's motive. They also knew that they would undoubtedly lose any battle unless the garrison was reinforced. Travis wrote to Fannin on March 3, begging one last time for reinforcements. He spoke of how "a blood-red banner waves from the church of Bejar, and in the camp above us, in token that the war is one of vengeance." In an attack, he knew that "the garrison would be put to the sword" but vowed that this

The red flag that Travis wrote about to Fannin hung from the tower of San Fernando Church *(above center)* in the heart of San Antonio.

did not frighten him or the other defenders and would only "make all fight with desperation."

Flying a red flag in time of war meant that no prisoners would be taken and no mercy shown. Anyone who tried to surrender or escape would be killed. The flag had flown since the first day of the siege. Santa Anna wrote in his autobiography that he had offered the chance for surrender and been rebuffed by Travis, who replied that he "would rather die than surrender to the Mexicans." No other accounts indicate that Santa Anna and Travis had any contact with each other. In fact, the Texians had little incentive to surrender. Santa Anna had already made it clear that all Anglos would be killed. Travis had also made it clear to the defenders that surrender would never be an option. In his earlier letter to Fannin on February 12, he wrote, "We consider death preferable to disgrace, which would be the result of giving up a Post which has been so dearly won."

> "We consider death preferable to disgrace, which would be the result of giving up a Post which has been so dearly won."
> —**William Barret Travis, 1846**

HOPES DASHED

David Crockett wrote what must have been the thoughts of all the men as the siege dragged on. They knew that their loved ones were dreading the news that would come with battle. "Those who fight the battles," he wrote in his journal on February 28, "experience but a small part of the privation, suffering, and anguish that follow in the train of ruthless war." On February 29, he wrote of seeing a portion of the Mexican troops heading in the direction of Goliad. "We think that he [Santa Anna] must have received news of Colonel Fanning's [Fannin] coming to our relief," he wrote. "We are all in high spirits." Those high spirits were soon dashed. On March 3, Crockett wrote, "We have given over all hopes of receiving assistance from Goliad." Two days later, he made his last entry into the journal: "March 5. Pop, pop, pop! Bom, bom, bom! throughout the day. No time for memorandums now. Go ahead! Liberty and independence for ever!" They were the last written words of any of the defenders.

On that same day, Santa Anna issued his general order at two in the afternoon. The assault took place before light the next morning. The artillery attacks and musical barrage that had annoyed the defenders stopped. The defenders inside the fort must have known that this signaled that the attack would come soon.

> "Great God, Sue! The Mexicans are inside our walls! All is lost! If they spare you, love our child!"
>
> —Lieutenant Almeron Dickinson, to his wife, Susanna, March 6, 1836

CHAPTER SIX

THE BATTLE

After the days of waiting, the fighting was over in a shockingly short time. "About three quarters of an hour of sustained firing was followed by a horrible steel arm combat," wrote one anonymous Mexican officer in a letter home. It was followed, he wrote, "by a painful but deserved carnage on the ungrateful colonists...Miserable ones! They no longer exist. All of them died—all of them!"

THE FATEFUL HOUR

"One hour! One short hour filled with such sublime struggle as has not been witnessed often in the brief compass of sixty minutes," wrote Cyrus Brady sixty-six years later. Sublime as it may have seemed, no one knows exactly what happened in that short hour after dawn on March 6, 1836. We know from Santa Anna's timetable and report that the battle was over quickly. But the accounts left behind by the Mexican officers are confusing. The only existing accounts of the defenders of the fort come from the few noncombatants whom Santa Anna allowed to leave after the fighting was done. He wanted them to carry his message to Sam Houston and others who might attempt to defy his authority.

> "One hour! One short hour filled with such sublime struggle as has not been witnessed often in the brief compass of sixty minutes."
>
> —Cyrus Brady, 1902, remembering the Alamo

Santa Anna's own report of his victory, dated the day of the battle, claims that his soldiers had achieved a victory that was "the most complete and glorious one in history." He further claims that they killed over six hundred defenders of the fort, with a loss to their forces of only seventy dead and three hundred wounded.

Santa Anna's estimates are grossly inaccurate. The fort was defended by no more than 260 men. Most historians agree that Santa Anna's forces took heavy losses, perhaps as many as one-third of his soldiers. The mayor of Bexar, Francisco Ruiz, witnessed the charge of the Mexican soldados. He said that in that early portion of the battle alone, "of eight hundred men, 130 were only left alive." Later, he was ordered to arrange the burial of Santa Anna's dead, and he wrote that there were about 1,600 of them.

It was a frenzied fight. According to historian John Meyers, "There was no thought of parley on either side. The Texians never doubted that there was only a choice between being slain in combat and being assassinated. The Mexicans on their part were worked up to a pitch of rage which admitted no pause to talk things over." Part of the Mexican rage came from the Texians' refusal to give up. However, even if they had attempted to surrender, they would certainly have been killed. Travis had pledged that his men "would make the Mexican victory so expensive, it would be worse than a defeat."

TAKING THE OUTER WALLS

The Alamo defenders had proved Travis correct. They had managed to fend off several assaults before the outer walls were breached. The soldados suffered terrible losses. "It was a victory of sheer numbers,"

David Crockett *(standing center)* and his fellow Alamo defenders make their last stand over the wall of the Alamo.

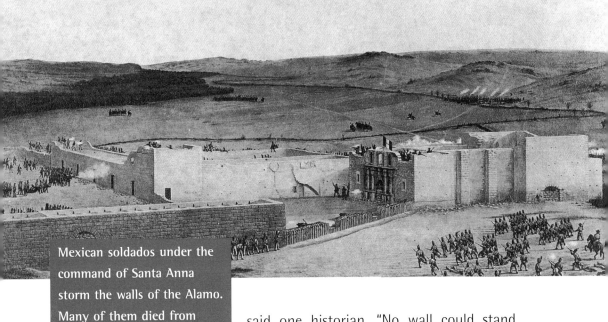

Mexican soldados under the command of Santa Anna storm the walls of the Alamo. Many of them died from friendly fire (Mexican shots).

said one historian. "No wall could stand against an army ready to sacrifice thousands." The Mexican soldiers may have had further incentive to clear the walls. They were being fired on by their own troops. Historians dispute whether this was deliberate or accidental. Santa Anna's orders to his elite reserve troops, which he sent forward as the initial charges failed, were to clear the walls of the Texian defenders. The general certainly knew that the reserves, shooting from where they were positioned, would hit other Mexicans. Most of their attack would fall not on the wall but on the soldados fighting below. Of the Mexican soldiers killed in the taking of the outer walls, perhaps less than "a fourth of [the deaths] were the result of enemy fire." Santa Anna achieved his goal of motivating the soldados to get over the walls, if only to keep them from being killed by their own countrymen.

The ferocity of the Mexican assault meant that the walls of the Alamo were breached. But breaching the walls would not end the

The Alamo was a bloody battle in which most of the deaths were caused by hand-to-hand combat. This depiction is by early twentieth-century artist Percy Moran.

fighting. With the Mexicans inside the walls, "The Texians fought like devils. It was at short range—muzzle to muzzle, hand to hand musket and rifle, bayonet and [B]owie knife.... The crush of firearms, the shouts of defiance, the cries of the dying and wounded.... The Texians defended desperately every inch of the fort." As the defenders fell, the Mexican soldados moved forward. They killed everyone in their path. In these close quarters, many defenders suffered multiple bayonet wounds and bled to death. Each defender was located and killed.

THE LAST GOOD-BYES

Amid the fighting, Lieutenant Almeron Dickinson rushed into the chapel where his wife and child were hiding. They were among the very few family members of Alamo defenders who had stayed in the fort. Dickinson had been a blacksmith in civilian life and was in charge of artillery at the Alamo. He knew the cause was lost, and he wanted to say good-bye to his wife. She would later report that he said, "Great God, Sue! The Mexicans are inside our walls! All is lost! If they spare you, love our child!" Dickinson then kissed his wife and rushed back to the fighting, where he was killed.

After the battle ended, many stories were told about the defenders. Many of them involved David Crockett. Some historians maintain he died in the fighting. Others say that he was executed by direct order of Santa Anna

In this version of David Crockett's death by W. H. Drake, Crockett dies before a Mexican firing squad.

after the fighting ended. Those who say he was executed divide again. Some claim he met death bravely. Others claim he pleaded for his life.

One account comes from Rafael Saldana, a Mexican cavalry commander. He wrote that "Kwockey [Crockett] was killed in a room of the mission. He stood on the inside . . . of the door and plunged his long knife into the bosom of every soldier that tried to enter." Eventually he was shot, an injury that broke his knife arm. He continued to fight back, swinging his musket around. Saldana said "a volley [round] was fired almost point blank and the last defender of the Alamo fell forward dead."

> "Kwockey [Crockett] was killed in a room of the mission. He stood on the inside . . . of the door and plunged his long knife into the bosom of every soldier that tried to enter."
>
> —Rafael Saldana, 1836

Disputing that account is the diary of Mexican officer Jose Enrique de la Peña. He stated that five or six of the defenders, including Crockett, survived the attack. Surrounded by the soldados, they surrendered. Peña claimed that the men were brought before Santa Anna and executed. He also indicated that Santa Anna was furious that his orders to kill everyone and not allow anyone to surrender had been disobeyed. Variations on this account range from Crockett begging for his life to Crockett lunging at Santa Anna and trying to kill him. However, as the Peña diary was found relatively recently, some historians doubt that it is a true document of the time.

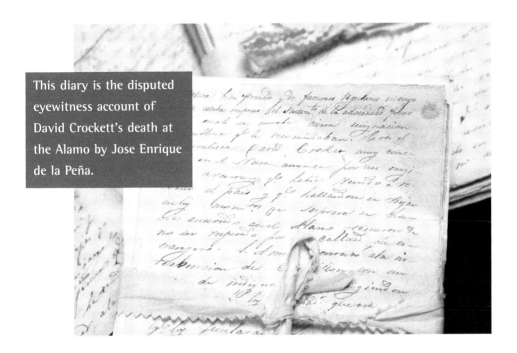

This diary is the disputed eyewitness account of David Crockett's death at the Alamo by Jose Enrique de la Peña.

Jim Bowie also was awarded a legendary death story. His biographer claimed that the Mexicans found him lying on his cot "with a brace of pistols in each hand, and a knife by his side. As the attackers rushed toward him, firing at close range and bayoneting him, the Bowie pistols fired and his famous Bowie knife went into action." He killed several attackers before he died. His biographer also recorded his mother's reaction to the news of her son's death. She reportedly said, "I'll wager no wounds were found in his back."

In other words, he would not have tried to run away, a tribute to his courage and bravery. Interestingly, most historians feel that Bowie had the least to lose of all the Alamo defenders. Apparently, he was suffering from advanced tuberculosis. Most historians think that he was dying and realized it before the fighting began. Killed at the Alamo, he became a legend, which would not have happened had he died from his illness.

LINE IN THE SAND

Facing certain death, why didn't the common soldiers—those not making the big decisions—just leave the Alamo? Historians have no way of knowing whether Santa Anna would have allowed a large group of the defenders to leave the Alamo unharmed. But at least one Alamo defender did decide to go.

Louis Rose was a former French soldier with a great deal of military experience who had settled in Texas several years before. He is thought to have come to the Alamo with his friend Jim Bowie.

Rose said that some unrest had arisen among the defenders as the siege dragged on. Some began to talk of escaping before the attack. According to Rose, Travis gathered all the defenders together. He gave a speech encouraging the men. As he concluded, he took his sword and drew a line in the sand. Then he asked the defenders to cross the line if they would stand with him to defend the Alamo. Everyone in the fort except Louis Rose stepped over the line *(below)*. Even Jim Bowie, too ill to leave the cot on which he had been brought to the meeting, asked to be carried across the line. Louis Rose slipped away that night and so survived the attack that came just a few days later.

Since everyone died, there is no way of knowing which of the stories (if any) are true. We only know what Susanna Dickinson later told a news reporter as she left the fort, she recalled, "I recognized Col. Crockett lying dead and mutilated between the church and two story barrack building, and even remember seeing his peculiar cap lying by his side."

THE FEW SURVIVORS

Susanna Dickinson and her daughter were the only Anglo survivors. They, along with Travis's slave, Joe, were treated honorably by Santa Anna. After questioning, he gave them some money and supplies and sent them away to deliver a message to the Texian leaders. Santa Anna hoped that after hearing what had happened at the Alamo, the rebelling Texians would be so frightened that they would give up any idea of further revolution.

Susanna Dickinson, wife of Almeron Dickinson, and her daughter were the only Anglo survivors of the siege of the Alamo.

BURNING THE DEAD

Francisco Ruiz, the mayor of San Antonio de Bexar, identified the bodies of Travis, Bowie, and Crockett for Santa Anna. The general ordered Ruiz to help with burning the bodies of the Alamo defenders and the burial of Santa Anna's casualties. Ruiz was able to provide information on how many of the soldados the Alamo defenders had been able to kill. He also is the source for the number of Alamo defenders whose bodies were burned—182.

The bodies had been gathered by the soldiers and placed in two piles. Lieutenant Colonel Peña recorded in his diary that he witnessed the burning. "The bodies," he wrote in his diary, "with their blackened and bloody faces disfigured by desperate death, their hair and uniforms burning at once, presented a dreadful and truly hellish sight."

A year later, the ashes of the defenders were collected "in a coffin, neatly covered with black and having the names of Travis, Bowie, and Crockett engraved on the inside of the lid, and carried to Bexar and placed in the parish church, where the Texian flag, a rifle and a sword were laid upon it." At the internment, Colonel Seguín saluted the dead. "These hallowed relics," he said, "are all that remains of those heroic men who so nobly fell, valiantly defending yon tower of the Alamo."

> "These hallowed relics are all that remains of those heroic men who so nobly fell, valiantly defending yon tower of the Alamo."
>
> **—Juan Seguín, 1837**

Sam Houston told another story. Travis had indicated that he would fire signal guns every morning to let people know that the fort still held. Houston went out each morning to listen for the sound. Of the morning the Alamo fell, he wrote, "I listened with acuteness of sense . . . waiting a signal of life or death from brave men. I listened in vain. Not the faintest murmur came floating on the calm morning air. I knew the Alamo had fallen."

"... contrary to every pledge given them, contrary to the rules of war, and contrary to every principle of humanity."

—Sam Houston, commenting on Goliad in a letter to General Santa Anna, 1842

CHAPTER SEVEN

GOLIAD MASSACRE

Texians and people throughout the United States were shocked as news of the carnage at the Alamo reached them. However, the most horrifying event was yet to come. People could question the decisions that led to the siege of the Alamo. But the massacre at Goliad, on the other hand, violated every code of war. It was an atrocity by any definition. It was, as Sam Houston noted in a letter to Santa Anna some years later, "contrary to every pledge given them [the Texian volunteers at Goliad], contrary to the rules of war, and contrary to every principle of humanity." It came about, in part, because Colonel Fannin was smart enough not to make the same mistakes that Travis had made.

THE TEXIAN ARMY ON THE MARCH

News of what had happened at the Alamo spread quickly. Texian soldiers in the area prepared to retreat and regroup in the face of the Mexican attack. Colonel Fannin was secure at Goliad. His men were anxious to fight the army that had defeated the Texian forces at the Alamo. Fannin decided to wait for orders before taking action.

As the Mexican army neared, Fannin feared a siege such as the one at the Alamo. On March 19, he ordered his men to retreat. The retreat was poorly organized and poorly executed. The men were overloaded with equipment and lacked the carts needed to transport their supplies and artillery. Fannin and his troops did not believe the Mexicans would follow them, but in fact, the Mexican general

The church *(below)* inside the walls of the fortress at Goliad as it looked in 1936, one hundred years after the fall of the Alamo.

was close behind. Caught in an open field not far from Coleto Creek, Fannin and his Texians prepared for the Mexican attack.

Historians dispute how many Mexicans attacked Fannin's troops, but clearly the Texians were outnumbered. They fought bravely and were able to withstand repeated attacks by the soldados. As the fighting wound down at day's end, the Texians had not been defeated. They could claim this as a victory of sorts. Without reinforcements of men and supplies, however, they could not continue. Their ammunition was running low. More important, they were separated from sources of water. They needed water not just for themselves and the care of the wounded. They also needed it to cool the cannons if fighting was to continue in the morning.

DECISION TO SURRENDER

Surrounded, unable to escape, and lacking water for his men, Fannin made the prudent decision. He requested surrender terms, asking in writing that he and his men be treated as prisoners of war. According to the standard treatment of prisoners at that time, his soldiers would be paroled. They would give their promise not to fight against this enemy in the future. Then they would be exiled to U.S. territory.

The Mexican commander was General José de Urrea. He faced a dilemma in responding to Fannin's request for surrender terms. He knew that Santa Anna had ordered that all prisoners were to be executed. Santa Anna had followed that policy himself at the Alamo. If Urrea did not accept the surrender, the Mexican forces would eventually win when the Texians ran out of ammunition. But his army would pay a terrible cost in lives while the fighting continued.

People disagree about whether Urrea acted honorably when he accepted Fannin's surrender. He did add to the written terms the phrase "at the disposal of the Supreme Mexican Government." Urrea later claimed that Fannin should have known from those words that he was not promising him any mercy. However, it is equally true he personally assured Fannin that the government would not execute a prisoner of war. Urrea assured Fannin that he expected Santa Anna would accept the terms. Fannin accepted the terms, and his troops surrendered.

The men were marched back to Goliad as prisoners of war. About 230 of them were well enough to make the march. Another 50 or so were transported back to the fort over the next several days. General Urrea remained in the field and did not return to Goliad.

However, he did write to Santa Anna requesting clemency for the prisoners. Urrea wrote that he thought he had protected them. Given the number of prisoners, he felt that Santa Anna would realize he could not kill them all. "I never thought," he wrote, "that the horrible spectacle of that massacre could take place in cold blood and without immediate urgency, a deed proscribed by the laws of war and condemned by the civilization of our country." It would seem that he misjudged the vindictiveness and brutality of his commander. On March 25, Santa Anna sent an order to Colonel Nicolás de la Portilla, in charge of the prisoners at Goliad, ordering their execution.

> "I never thought that the horrible spectacle of that massacre could take place in cold blood and without immediate urgency, a deed proscribed by the laws of war and condemned by the civilization of our country."
>
> —José de Urrea, 1836

Colonel Nicolás de la Portilla, shown here in the 1850s or 1860s, was in charge of the prisoners at Goliad.

MERCY OR DEATH?

Colonel Portilla recorded in his diary the conflicting orders he received from the two commanders. Urrea, he confirmed, had told him to put the prisoners to work but not to mistreat them in any way. Portilla's orders from Santa Anna were to execute the men. In his diary entry for March 27, Portilla recorded his decision "to carry out the orders of the general-in-chief because I considered them superior [since Santa Anna outranked Urrea]."

On Sunday, March 27, the prisoners were lined up. John C. Duval was one of the few Texians to survive the massacre. He later wrote that they were told they were being taken to boats that would transport them to New Orleans. Joseph Spohn, saved from execution because he had medical skills needed by the Mexicans, confirmed that in his account. The Texians, he said, were "full of hope that they were to be shipped to the United States, which had been promised." The Mexicans marched them out of the fort in three separate groups.

The three groups were taken along paths that separated them from one another's view. At some point, the men were ordered to halt and told to sit down. As they did so, the Mexican soldados escorting them opened fire with their rifles. The men could not escape.

This painting by Sam Houston's son shows the Mexican army under the comand of Colonel Nicolás de la Portilla marching the Texians out of Goldiad in three groups to be slaughtered.

WAITING FOR NEWS OF TEXAS INDEPENDENCE

We take instant communication for granted. We know we can watch news from around the world twenty-four hours a day, seven days a week, and 365 days a year. But the soldiers defending the Alamo had to depend on messengers to get their news.

After the capture of the Alamo from the Mexicans in December 1835, political leaders in Texas decided that a representative group of Texians should meet at a convention to decide how to protect the Texian settlers. Forty-four men were selected to meet at Washington-on-the-Brazos (present day Washington, Texas). There, they declared their independence from Mexico on March 2, 1836. A new flag *(right)* flew to commemorate the event.

Santa Anna's assault on the Alamo took place on the morning of March 6. The Alamo defenders knew that the convention was meeting. David Crockett's journal indicated that they expected the convention to vote for independence. The news of the vote never reached the Alamo, however. None of the defenders lived to know that Texas was independent.

Communication is extremely important in wartime, but during the Texas Revolution, messengers carried written orders from the commander to his subordinates. Then they returned with any reply. This meant that a week or more could pass before a local officer received a decision from his commander. Because of this, local commanders had a great deal of autonomy. They were expected to make their own decisions.

The system worked well enough most of the time. It failed with a commander such as Colonel Fannin. He was so indecisive that he always wanted to wait for direct orders from the commander in chief. Twice Fannin faced situations requiring him to make a decision on his own. In both cases, his inability to decide had fatal results. The first prevented the Alamo defenders from receiving relief and supplies. The second cost him his own life.

THE SLAUGHTER

"Most of them, frozen in astonishment, simply stood there and were slaughtered," noted one historian. Then the soldiers used their bayonets on the bodies, "lunging at everything that twitched." One of the three groups, however, had a better chance of survival.

John Duval wrote that he first knew what was happening when he suddenly heard firing from the two directions where the other groups had marched. "Some one near me exclaimed, 'Boys, they are going to shoot us!' and . . . I heard the clicking of musket locks. The man in front of me was shot dead, and in falling he knocked me down." Falling down probably saved Duval's life. He estimated that only about two-thirds of the column he was in died in the first volley, perhaps because they had some warning of what was happening. Those still standing tried to run away,

More than 250 men were killed at Goliad. This is an early twentieth-century engraving by Norman Price.

and the Mexican soldados chased after them. That gave Duval the chance to escape.

Crossing a nearby river, he met two others who had escaped. They saw a party of Mexican soldiers headed their way on horseback, but the soldados had not seen them. Another group of about five Texians had been spotted. Duval wrote that he and the other two watched helplessly as the Mexicans "charged upon them . . . [and] speared them to death."

Within the fort, those men who had been unable to march out with the others were brought into the courtyard on their stretchers and executed there. Joseph Spohn was sent to fetch Fannin, who had a severe thigh wound from the fighting at Coleto. Fannin hobbled out into the courtyard. A chair was brought for him to sit on, since he was unable to stand. Spohn recorded that he "appeared resolute and firm." Fannin was blindfolded and a volley of musket fire sent him to join his troops.

The bodies of the slain soldiers were piled and burned. Many believe that some of those men were still alive. Amazingly, twenty-eight Texians had managed to get away in the chaos of the firing. The stories they told of what happened to those who didn't escape enraged the Texians, galvanized the fight for independence, and caused Mexico to lose Texas forever.

The phrase that resounds through U.S. history may indeed be "Remember the Alamo." But for sheer horror, the events at Goliad had an equal impact on the decisions that led to Texas independence and eventual union with the United States.

> " [I]n a short time they were running like turkeys, whipped and discomfited."
>
> —Walter P. Lane, 1836

CHAPTER EIGHT

THE BATTLE OF SAN JACINTO

Many of the Texian leaders had been disappointed by the unwillingness of the settlers to rise up and defend their own territory. Sam Houston had put out a strong call to arms on March 2, 1836, right after Texas declared independence from Mexico. On that date, even before the Alamo fell, he demanded that "the citizens of Texas must rally to the aid of our army, or it will perish.... The enemy must be driven from our soil." But even this call to arms was not successful.

Santa Anna had noticed the reluctance of the average settlers to defend Texian independence. He felt it showed that most Texians wanted to remain part of Mexico. It confirmed his belief that outside agitators from the United States caused the rebellion in Texas.

A Panicked Retreat

The immediate result of the execution of Fannin's soldiers at Goliad was that many of the soldiers still in the army went home. They gathered their families and began to leave the area. Houston tried to maintain an orderly retreat with the remains of his army. Fighting with this retreating army was Captain Juan Seguín, Travis's messenger from the Alamo. He had raised a company of thirty-seven militiamen who served with the Texas military under Houston's command.

> "[T]he citizens of Texas must rally to the aid of our army, or it will perish. . . . The enemy must be driven from our soil."
>
> —Sam Houston, March 2, 1836

As his army retreated, Houston announced that he could not protect the villages left behind army lines from the advancing Mexican army. With that announcement, the orderly retreat degenerated into a panic. It is known to Texas history as the Runaway Scrape. People left every-

The Hazards of Life on the Frontier

Living on the frontier was dangerous. Pioneers accepted that danger was part of their everyday lives. Those who could not live with that didn't become settlers. Many who tested the frontier's challenges returned to civilization after a few months or years rather than endure the hardships.

The Runaway Scrape was an escape from a different kind of danger. Whole communities were trying to get away from possible slaughter by the Mexican army. In modern times, refugee camps all over the world hold people who have escaped invading armies.

thing behind in their rush to get away before capture by the Mexican army. They often left unprepared for the hardships of the trail. The weather was cold, and many people did not carry enough food. The result was a trail of dead bodies along the path of retreat. Dilue Rose Harris was ten years old in 1836. Her family spent six weeks away from home during the Runaway Scrape. "We left home at sunset, hauling clothes, bedding and provisions," she remembered later. "Mother and I were walking, she with an infant in her arms." No one could go home unless Santa Anna and his army were stopped.

Santa Anna consolidated his position. He was sure that the Texians were just going to keep running. On April 18, a courier of the Mexican army was captured. Houston found out that advancing Mexicans were within striking range of his troops. He ordered a forced march on the morning of April 19 to reach a critical ferry crossing on the San Jacinto River before the Mexicans could arrive. He later reported, "We continued to march through the night, making but one halt in the prairie for a short time, and without refreshments." He had left all his sick and all his supplies behind in order to move the army quickly.

> "We continued to march through the night, making but one halt in the prairie for a short time, and without refreshments."
>
> —Sam Houston, April 25, 1836

When the Texian army finally arrived at Lynch's Ferry, Houston learned that Santa Anna and the Mexican army were fast approaching. He quickly searched the area and selected a location that looked defensible. The two armies met and skirmished on April 20 and then encamped less than a mile from each other. They did not resume fighting the next morning. Both leaders chose to rest their soldiers.

Santa Anna, however, was apparently either overconfident or careless. He failed to post guards while his soldiers rested on April 21. Houston took advantage of the situation. He ordered an attack during the Mexican siesta (rest time) at midafternoon.

THE TEXIANS REVENGE

The Texian troops went into battle shouting, "Remember the Alamo!" Walter P. Lane was one of the Texian soldiers attacking that day at San Jacinto. "We never fired a gun till we got within forty yards," he remembered. "In a second we were into them with guns, pistols, and [B]owie knives . . . in a short time they were running like turkeys, whipped and discomfited."

Lane also recalled an incident in which some escaping Mexican soldados were attempting to get across the river. "Some

The Battle of San Jacinto became a day of revenge for the Texian troops. They slaughtered hundreds of Mexican soldiers as payback for the Alamo and Goliad.

one cried for us to stop firing. We did so. He hailed the Mexicans in Spanish and told them to come back and we would not hurt them. They returned, and as they neared the shore, he said, 'Now, boys, give it to them,' which they did, killing some two hundred." Added Lane, "I never fired a shot."

It would not be the first (or last) instance in U.S. history when soldiers in battle did not follow the rules of war. There are, unfortunately, always individuals who will take advantage of the situation. Lane does not say what, if anything, was done to the soldier who gave the order. However, another historian puts the event in context. "It was a credit to the Texan officers," he wrote, "that there were 730 prisoners at the end of that bloody afternoon." This was a far different outcome than the Texians experienced at the Alamo and at Goliad.

Santa Anna Caught Napping

It is also a tribute to the self-control of the officers that Santa Anna, caught napping under a tree, was not in any way injured. He was taken prisoner without incident. He later spoke of his surprise at the courtesy Houston extended to him.

Santa Anna claimed that Houston's victory came because the Mexicans were badly outnumbered. In fact, the reverse was true. Houston later described his diminished forces as exhausted from forced marches in the rain on muddy roads. They were, he wrote, "badly supplied with rations and clothing, yet, amid every difficulty they bore up with cheerfulness and fortitude."

According to Houston's official report, the entire battle "lasted about eighteen minutes...until we were in possession of the enemy's encampment." He reports only two deaths on the battlefield, with six wounded soldiers dying later. He also reported more

Santa Anna *(center left in white trousers)* was brought before Sam Houston *(lying down)*, where he surrendered. Houston was lying down because he had been injured at the Battle of San Jacinto.

than six hundred Mexican deaths and two hundred wounded. After all the Texians had been through, it was an easy victory.

Houston and Santa Anna signed a treaty that gave the province of Texas its independence. Houston decided that Santa Anna should be sent to Washington, D.C., to talk with President Andrew Jackson before being released. This was a political ploy on the part of Houston. He wanted the United States to be reassured that Santa Anna would leave the Texians alone. Many existing accounts describe Santa Anna's trip to meet the president. All of them make it clear that, although he was treated as the visiting head of state of Mexico, he remained a prisoner. He was even escorted home by the U.S. Navy after his visit. In Santa Anna's version of the event, however, Houston is his great friend. Houston asks him as a special favor to go to Washington.

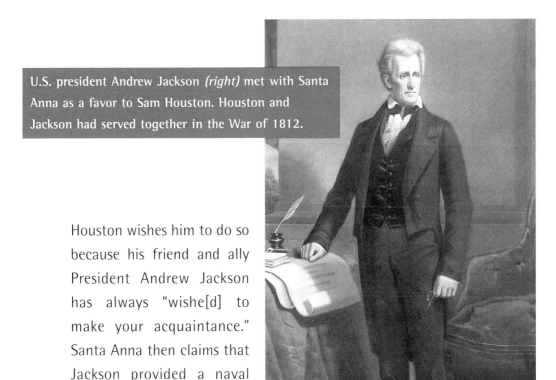

Houston wishes him to do so because his friend and ally President Andrew Jackson has always "wishe[d] to make your acquaintance." Santa Anna then claims that Jackson provided a naval vessel simply to make his journey home easier.

Dilue Rose Harris and her family, still on the Runaway Scrape, heard the news of Houston's victory over Santa Anna at (appropriately) the town of Liberty. Their route home took them through the San Jacinto battlefield on April 26. "We had to pass among the dead Mexicans," Harris would remember, "and father pulled one out of the road, so we could get by without driving over the body." It was not a pleasant memory for a girl who would celebrate her eleventh birthday two days later.

The Texas Revolution was over. Begun in October 1835, the entire war lasted only six months. The story, of course, didn't end with the defeat of Santa Anna at San Jacinto. The real conflict would not be resolved until the end of yet another war still ten years in the future—the Mexican-American War (1846–1848). However, that war would be fought with the power of the United States and a professional army.

The revolution had freed the Texians from the tyranny of Santa Anna. It had also provided an image of the Alamo defenders that was spoken of with pride throughout the United States, a country that did not send soldiers to take part in the six-month war.

> "... all freemen and lovers of freedom in the world must reverence and adore—the American Union."
> —Anson Jones, president of the Republic of Texas, 1846

CHAPTER NINE

INDEPENDENCE AND STATEHOOD

On March 2, 1836, Texas declared independence from Mexico. The men who died defending the Alamo did not know that they had given their lives for the new Republic of Texas. Although independence had been declared, it took the Texians' decisive victory at San Jacinto to make it a reality.

THE REPUBLIC OF TEXAS

After the defeat of Santa Anna at San Jacinto, Sam Houston was elected the first president of the Republic of Texas. He immediately began the process that led to Texas joining the United States. The

On March 2, 1836, a group of Texians signed the Declaration of Independence from Mexico *(right)*. Sam Houston was elected the first president of the Republic of Texas. Mexico did not recognize the new republic.

process was neither quick nor easy, however. Houston's friend, President Andrew Jackson, who supported the idea of annexing Texas, was completing his term in office. There was much indignation in the United States at Mexico for the suffering of the Texians. Newspapers railed against the defeat at the Alamo and the cruelty of Santa Anna. The *New York Post* wrote of the tremendous support many people had for Texas because Santa Anna had not followed "the rules of civilized warfare." The result of his brutality, they editorialized, had been "to awaken the general sympathy" and encourage "ardent spirits to throng to the aid of their brethren."

The U.S. population might have been sympathetic to the plight of the Texians. But admitting them to statehood was another matter. Serious political debate was going on over the issue of slavery. Texas was a large slaveholding territory. Several states could possibly be carved from its territory. That many new slave states would severely upset the balance of congressmen representing slaveholding and slave-free states in Congress.

There were other issues as well. President Jackson had offered several times to purchase Texas from Mexico for as much as four million dollars. Those offers had been rebuffed by the Mexican government as insulting. The Mexican government had long claimed that the Texas independence movement was actually a land grab by the U.S. government disguised as a local dispute over constitutional rights. For Texas to be admitted then as a part of the United States would make it appear that the revolution had been just an excuse to acquire Texas. If Texas quickly became a state, it was fairly certain that the United States would face attack by Santa Anna's army. The Texas statehood quest called for caution on the part of the United States.

Jackson's government officially recognized Texas as an independent republic. But he could do no more before leaving office. Texas president Houston petitioned for annexation under Jackson's successor, Martin Van Buren, but Van Buren was not willing to take up the cause of Texas statehood.

The Texians next tried to get a direct congressional resolution in support of annexation. But former president John Quincy Adams led the opposition in Congress to prevent its passage.

Former president John Quincy Adams, shown here in a photograph from the mid-1800s, opposed the annexation of Texas while he was a member of Congress (1830–1848).

In 1838 Houston gave up his attempts to have the Texas territory annexed to the United States. Houston's successor as president of the Texas Republic, Mirabeau Lamar, did not even try. (Under the Republic of Texas, presidents could not succeed themselves. That meant the holder of the office changed every two years.)

THE UNITED STATES GOES TO WAR FOR TEXAS

In 1841 Sam Houston became president of the republic again, and John Tyler took office as president of the United States. Houston began a bold policy. He made it clear that Texas needed the support of a major power. Since the United States had rejected it, Texas looked into aligning itself with either Great Britain or France to defend its interests. In 1842, after Mexico made two more attempts to invade Texas, the United States suddenly felt the need to respond. U.S. leaders figured it was better to have Texas as part of the United States than to let it either be reabsorbed into Mexico or controlled by a European nation.

As a U.S. presidential election took place in 1844, the topic that elected James K. Polk instead of Henry Clay

James K. Polk *(right)* won the presidential election in part because he stood firmly behind annexing Texas.

Anson Jones *(left)* was president of Texas in 1845 when Texas elected to become part of the United States.

was his stand for the annexation of Texas. Congress passed a joint resolution on February 28, 1845, in favor of annexation. Then the statehood debate went back to Texas. Houston was no longer president. The current president, Anson Jones, called a convention to decide the issue. On December 29, 1845, Texas elected to become the twenty-eighth state in the United States.

Mexico responded by declaring war. Mexico wanted Texas back. President James K. Polk announced the U.S. intention to keep Texas, to set the boundary with Mexico at the Rio Grande, and to purchase California. Thus the Mexican-American War began on April 25, 1846. Although outnumbered in every engagement, the United States defeated Santa Anna and his forces time and time again and forced them to retreat. Santa Anna, defeated at Buena Vista, Mexico, in February 1847 by a force one-third the size of his army, continued the fight. The U.S. forces captured Mexico City in September 1847. Santa Anna regrouped and attacked again but

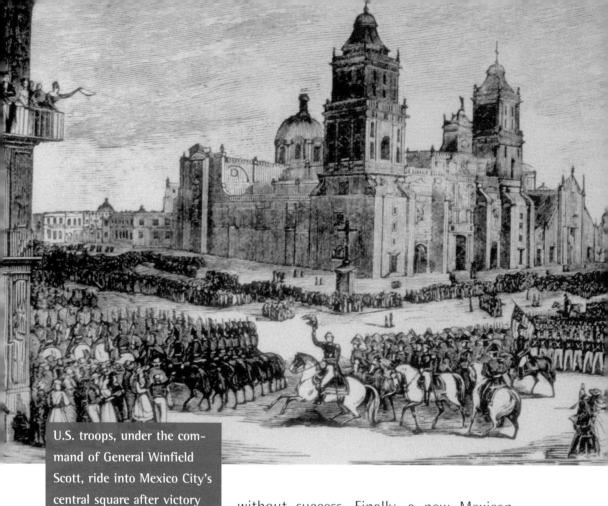

U.S. troops, under the command of General Winfield Scott, ride into Mexico City's central square after victory in the Mexican-American War in 1848.

without success. Finally, a new Mexican government was formed in February 1848 that agreed to peace negotiations.

THE FINAL ALAMO VICTORY

At the signing of the Treaty of Guadalupe Hidalgo in 1848, ending the Mexican-American War, the United States kept Texas. It also gained territories that included California, Arizona, and the parts of New Mexico, Utah, Nevada, and Colorado that had not been included in the Louisiana Purchase. The Rio Grande became the boundary between the United States and Mexico. The United States owned territory from the Atlantic Ocean to the Pacific Ocean.

REMEMBERING TEXIAN HEROES

The Alamo story has long moved from historical reality to the greatest of legends. Sam Houston's call to his troops at San Jacinto to "Remember the Alamo"—or as some historians say, "Remember the Alamo! Remember Goliad"—echoes through national memory. The call to remember is invoked whenever Americans feel that the United States has been attacked and damaged unfairly and that the people need to respond. However, one side effect of all this remembering has been to turn the Alamo defenders into legendary icons rather than allow them to be the everyday people who chose to fight for their beliefs.

None of the Alamo defenders was born a hero. Each came to be in that fort for his own reasons. As the defenders were turned into legends, the real story that they can tell is sometimes lost. They were heroes not because they were perfect men but because they reacted bravely in a bad situation. Faced with certain death, they responded with fearlessness and courage *(below)*. The Texians were very human until the moment when their defense of their beliefs gave rise to a revolution.

The soldiers and frontiersmen who died in the Alamo represented a small proportion of those who died in the wars with Mexico. Still, more than 170 years later, their story still dominates the history of the time. Sam Houston said of the Alamo that "when the news of this act of cold-blooded barbarity flew through the colonies, it stirred up a spirit that would never sleep again." It certainly stirred up a people to fight and gain their independence.

Anson Jones was the last president of the Republic of Texas. As he turned over the government to the new state of Texas on February 19, 1846, he gave a speech for the occasion. In it he spoke of

Anson Jones lowers the Texas flag at the annexation ceremony on February 19, 1846.

the satisfaction he personally felt that Texas would "become fixed forever in that glorious constellation which all freemen and lovers of freedom in the world must reverence and adore—the American Union." Amid all his poetical oratory, however, he somberly remembered the "fields of carnage" that gave birth to the republic.

The Alamo that remains is a small fraction of the fort where those defenders gave their lives. But the early leaders of Texas as a republic and as a state were correct. The memory of the Alamo and its defenders has indeed remained strong, long after they were gone.

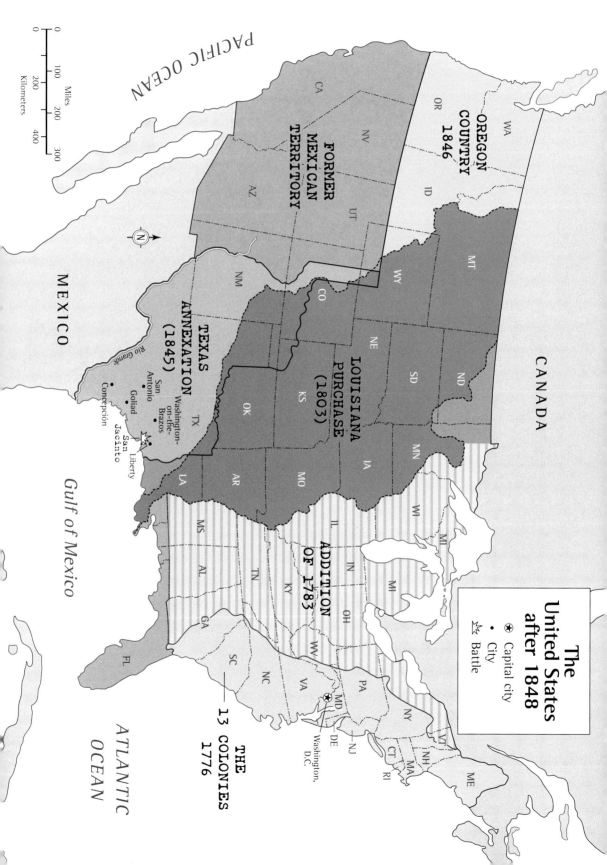

The United States
after 1848

Capital city ⊛
City •
Battle ⚔

PACIFIC OCEAN

OREGON
COUNTRY
1846

FORMER
MEXICAN
TERRITORY

TEXAS
ANNEXATION
(1845)

LOUISIANA
PURCHASE
(1803)

ADDITION
OF 1783

THE
13 COLONIES
1776

MEXICO

CANADA

Gulf of Mexico

ATLANTIC
OCEAN

Rio Grande

San Antonio
Goliad
Concepción
Washington-on-the-Brazos
San Jacinto
Liberty

Washington, D.C.

WA
OR
CA
NV
AZ
UT
ID
MT
WY
CO
NM
NE
SD
ND
KS
OK
TX
IA
MN
MO
AR
LA
WI
MI
IL
IN
KY
TN
MS
AL
GA
FL
SC
NC
VA
WV
OH
PA
NY
MD
DE
NJ
VT
NH
MA
RI
CT
ME

N

Miles
0   100   200   300
Kilometers
0   200   400

1810	Mexico declares independence from Spain.
1821	Mexico gains independence from Spain in Treaty of Córdoba.
1823	Stephen Austin and three hundred American families begin settlement of Texas.
1824	Mexico adopts a constitution for a republican form of government.
1830	Mexican government halts immigration of U.S. citizens to Mexico.
1833	Santa Anna is elected president of Mexico and gradually assumes power as a dictator.
1835	The first battle of the Texas Revolution occurs when citizens refuse to allow the cannon to be taken from Gonzales on October 3.
	The Battle of Concepción is fought on October 29.
	Texians besiege the Alamo. The fort is surrendered to them by Mexican General Cos in December.
1836	General Santa Anna and troops arrive on February 23 to begin the siege of Alamo.
	Delegates declare Texas independence from Mexico on March 2.
	The Alamo falls to Santa Anna on March 6.
	Colonel Fannin surrenders his forces at Coleto on March 20.

1836	Prisoners of war at Goliad are massacred on March 27.
	General Sam Houston defeats Santa Anna at San Jacinto on April 21 and takes him prisoner.
	On May 14, Treaties of Velasco are signed in which Santa Anna recognizes Texas independence.
1845	On December 29, Texas becomes a state.
1846	The Battle of Palo Alto leads the United States to declare war on Mexico.
1847	U.S. troops capture Mexico City.
1848	The United States and Mexico sign the Treaty of Guadalupe Hildago ending the Mexican-American War.

6 Albert Curtis, *Remember the Alamo* (San Antonio: Clegg Company, 1961), frontispiece.

9 Ibid.

10 Jacqueline Beretta Tomerlin, comp., *Fugitive Letters, 1829–1836 Stephen F. Austin to David G. Burnet* (San Antonio: Trinity University Press, 1981), 18.

16 Gregg Cantrell, *Stephen F. Austin: Empresario of Texas* (New Haven, CT: Yale University Press, 1999), 86.

17 Tomerlin, 18.

17 Cantrell, 86.

17–18 Eugene Campbell Barker, *The Life of Stephen F. Austin: Founder of Texas, 1793–1836* (Austin: Texas State Historical Association, 1925), 90.

18 Stephen F. Austin, *Establishing Austin's Colony: The First Book Printed in Texas, with the Laws, Orders and Contracts of Colonization* (1829; repr., Austin, TX: Pemberton Press, 1970), 33.

19 John J. Linn, *Reminiscences of Fifty Years in Texas* (New York: D. & J. Sadlier & Co., 1883), 50.

19 Barker, *The Life of Stephen F. Austin*, 104.

22 Tomerlin, *Fugitive Letters*, 35.

22 Eugene Campbell Barker, "The Organization of the Texas Revolution," *Publications of the Southern History Association* 5, no. 6 (November 1901): 459.

23 Eugene Campbell Barker, *Mexico and Texas 1821–1835* (1928; repr., New York: Russell & Russell, 1965), 100.

23 Linn, *Reminiscences of Fifty Years*, 50.

23 Ibid.

23 Jeff Long, *Duel of Eagles: The Mexican and U.S. Fight for the Alamo* (New York: William Morrow and Company, 1990), 111.

24 David Lee Child, *The Texan Revolution* (Washington, DC: J. & G. S. Gideon, Printers, 1843), 16.

25 Ann Fears Crawford, ed., *The Eagle: The Autobiography of Santa Anna* (Austin, TX: State House Press, 1988), 49.

25 H. W. Brands, *Lone Star Nations* (New York: Doubleday, 2004), 309.

25 John F. Rios, ed., *Readings on the Alamo* (New York: Vantage Press, 1987), 123.

25 Tomerlin, *Fugitive Letters*, 35.

25–26 Ibid.

28 Amelia W. Williams and Eugene C. Barker, eds, *The Writings of Sam Houston 1813–1863*, vol. 1 (Austin, TX: Jenkins Publishing Company, 1970), 317.

28 Barker, *The Life of Stephen F. Austin*, 426.

30 Virgil E. Baugh, *Rendezvous at the Alamo: Highlights in the Lives of Bowie, Crockett, and Travis* (New York: Pageant Press, 1960), 95.

33 Archie P. McDonald, *Travis* (Austin, TX: Jenkins Publishing Co., 1976), 13.

33 J. R. Edmondson, *The Alamo Story: From Early History to Current Conflicts* (Plano: Republic of Texas Press, 2000), 277.

33 McDonald, *Travis*, 14.

33 David Crockett, *Davy Crockett's Own Story As Written by Himself* (Philadelphia: G. G. Evans, 1860), 369.

34 Texas State Historical Society, *Handbook of Texas Online*, s.v.

"Bowie, James," April 12, 2004, http://www.tsha.utexas.edu/handbook/online/articles/BB/fbo45.html (January 26, 2006).

35 Baugh, 95.

36 Ibid.

36 *Handbook of Texas Online*, s.v. "Crockett, David," June 6, 2001, http://www.tsha.utexas.edu/handbook/online/articles/CC/fcr24.html (January 26, 2006).

36 Long, *Duel of Eagles*, 129.

39 James E. Crisp, *Sleuthing the Alamo* (New York: Oxford University Press, 2005), 61.

42 Crawford, *The Eagle*, 47–55.

42 Crockett, *Davy Crockett's Own Story*, 374–375.

43 Miguel A. Sánchez Lamego, *The Siege and Taking of the Alamo* (Santa Fe, NM: Press of the Territorian, 1968), 33.

43 Edmondson, *The Alamo Story*, 317.

45 Phil Rosenthal and Bill Groneman, *Roll Call at the Alamo* (Fort Collins, CO: Old Army Press, 1985), 40.

45 Ben H. Procter, *The Battle of the Alamo* (Austin: Texas State Historical Association, 1986), 9.

47 Ibid., 9.

49 Long, *Duel of Eagles*, 137, 139, 142.

50 Crawford, *The Eagle*, 50.

50 Lamego, 33.

50 James Wakefield Burke, *Missions of Old Texas* (Cranbury, NJ: A. S. Barnes and Co., 1971), 149.

51 Martha Anne Turner, *William Barret Travis: His Sword and His Pen* (Waco, TX: Texian Press, 1972), 229.

51 Edmondson, *The Alamo Story*, 304.

51 David Crockett, *Colonel Crockett's Exploits and Adventures in Texas* (New York: William H. Graham, 1848), 189.

52 Ibid.

53 Ibid., 195.

53 Ibid.

53 Crisp, *Sleuthing the Alamo*, 63.

54 Rosenthal and Groneman, *Roll Call at the Alamo*, 24.

54 Richard G. Santos, *Santa Anna's Campaign against Texas* (Waco, TX: Texian Press, 1968), 64.

54–55 Turner, 229.

55 Crawford, *The Eagle*, 51.

56 Wallace O. Chariton, *Exploring the Alamo Legends* (Dallas: Wordware Publishing, 1990), 86.

56 Ibid.

56 Crockett, *Colonel Crockett's Exploits*, 196–202.

58 C. Richard King, *Susanna Dickinson: Messenger of the Alamo* (Austin, TX: Shoal Creek Publishers, 1976), 41.

58 Rios, *Readings on the Alamo*, 116.

58 Cyrus Townsend Brady, *Border Fights & Fighters* (New York: McClure, Phillips & Co., 1902), 325.

59 Ibid.

59 Sánchez Lamego, *The Siege and Taking of the Alamo*, 36.

59 Timothy M. Matovina, *The Alamo Remembered: Tejano Accounts and Perspectives* (Austin: University of Texas Press, 1995), 43–44.

59–60 John M. Myers, *The Alamo* (New York: E. P. Dutton & Company, 1948), 220.

60 Walter A. Lord, *A Time to Stand* (New York: Harper & Brothers, 1961), 137.

61 Lon Tinkle, *13 Days to Glory: The Siege of the Alamo* (College Station: Texas A&M University Press, 1985), 207.

61 Stephen Hardin, *The Alamo 1836* (Westport, CT: Praeger, 2004), 41.

62 John S. Ford, *Origin and Fall of*

the Alamo (San Antonio: Johnson Brothers Printing Company, 1895), 20.

62 King, 41.

64 James T. DeShields, *Tall Men with Long Rifles: The Glamour Story of the Texas Revolution as Told by Captain Creed Taylor* (San Antonio: Naylor Printing Company, 1935), 163–164.

64 Ibid.

65 Clifford Hopewell, *James Bowie: Texas Fighting Man* (Austin, TX: Eakin Press, 1994), xv.

65 Ibid., 125.

67 Dan Kilgore, *How Did Davy Die?* (College Station: Texas A&M University Press, 1978), 40–41.

68 Hardin, *The Alamo*, 48.

68 A. Garland Adair and M. H. Crockett Sr., eds., *Heroes of the Alamo* (New York: Exposition Press, 1956), 72.

68 Ibid.

69 C. Richard King, *James Clinton Neill: The Shadow Commander of the Alamo* (Austin, TX: Eakin Press, 2002), 102.

70 Sam Houston, *Letter of General Sam Houston to General Santa Anna, 21 March 1842* (Washington, DC: Congressional Globe Office, 1852), 4.

70 Ibid.

73 Carlos E. Castañeda, *The Mexican Side of the Texan Revolution* (1928; repr., Austin, TX: Grapic Ideas, 1970), 242.

73 Ibid.

74 Ibid., 244.

75 Gary Brown, *Hesitant Martyr in the Texas Revolution: James Walker Fannin* (Plano: Republic of Texas Press, 2000), 220.

76 Donald Barr Chidsey, *The War with Mexico* (New York: Crown Publishers, 1968), 13.

76–77 Neil B. Carmony and David E. Brown, eds., *Tough Times in Rough Places: Personal Narratives of Adventure, Death, and Survival on the Western Frontier* (Salt Lake City: University of Utah Press, 2001), 20.

78 Ibid., 21.

78 Brown, *Hesitant Martyr*, 221.

79 Walter P. Lane, *The Adventures and Recollections of General Walter P. Lane, a San Jacinto Veteran* (Marshall, TX: Tri-Weekly Herald Job Print, 1887), 11.

79 Donald Day and Harry Herbert, eds., *Autobiography of Sam Houston* (Norman: University of Oklahoma Press, 1954), 99.

80 Ibid.

81 Lisa Waller Rogers, *A Texas Sampler: Historical Recollections* (Lubbock: Texas Tech University Press, 1998), 43.

81 Williams and Barker, *The Writings of Sam Houston*, 417.

81 Ibid.

82 Lane, 11.

83 Ibid., 12.

83 Chidsey, *The War with Mexico*, 38.

83 William H. Brooker, *Texas* (Columbus, OH: Press of Nitschke Brothers, 1897), 90.

83 Crawford, *The Eagle*, 56.

85 Williams and Barker, *The Writings of Sam Houston*, 419.

85 Rogers, *A Texas Sampler*, 47.

87 Anson Jones, *Valedictory Speech, February 19, 1846, Executive Record Book.* Austin: Texas State Library and Archives Commission, 521.

88 Lord, *A Time to Stand*, 169.

94 Day and Herbert, *Autobiography*, 102.

95 Jones, 521.

BIBLIOGRAPHY

Adair, A. Garland, and M. H. Crockett Sr., eds. *Heroes of the Alamo*. New York: Exposition Press, 1956.

Austin, Stephen F. *Establishing Austin's Colony: The First Book Printed in Texas, with the Laws, Orders and Contracts of Colonization*. 1829. Reprint, Austin, TX: Pemberton Press, 1970.

Barker, Eugene Campbell. *The Life of Stephen F. Austin: Founder of Texas, 1793–1836*. Austin: Texas State Historical Association, 1925.

——. *Mexico and Texas 1821–1835*. 1928. Reprint, New York: Russell & Russell, 1965.

——. "The Organization of the Texas Revolution." *Publications of the Southern History Association* 5, no. 6 (November 1901): 451–476.

Baugh, Virgil E. *Rendezvous at the Alamo: Highlights in the Lives of Bowie, Crockett, and Travis*. New York: Pageant Press, 1960.

Binkley, William C. *The Texas Revolution*. Baton Rouge: Louisiana State University Press, 1952.

Brady, Cyrus Townsend. *Border Fights & Fighters*. New York: McClure, Phillips & Co., 1902.

Brands, H. W. *Lone Star Nation*. New York: Doubleday, 2004.

Brooker, William H. *Texas*. Columbus, OH: Press of Nitschke Brothers, 1897.

Brown, Gary. *Hesitant Martyr in the Texas Revolution: James Walker Fannin*. Plano: Republic of Texas Press, 2000.

Brown, Kenneth. *The Last Day*. San Angelo, TX: Gemini Publications, 1986.

Burke, James Wakefield. *Missions of Old Texas*. Cranbury, NJ: A. S. Barnes and Co., 1971.

Cantrell, Gregg. *Stephen F. Austin: Empresario of Texas*. New Haven, CT: Yale University Press, 1999.

Carmony, Neil B., and David E. Brown, eds. *Tough Times in Rough Places: Personal Narratives of Adventure, Death, and Survival on the Western Frontier*. Salt Lake City: University of Utah Press, 2001.

Castañeda, Carlos E. *The Mexican Side of the Texan Revolution*. 1928. Reprint, Austin, TX: Graphic Ideas, 1970.

Chariton, Wallace O. *Exploring the Alamo Legends*. Dallas: Wordware Publishing, 1990.

Chidsey, Donald Barr. *The War with Mexico*. New York: Crown Publishers, 1968.

Child, David Lee. *The Texan Revolution*. Washington, DC: J. & G. S. Gideon, Printers, 1843.

Cobia, Manley F., Jr. *Journey into the Land of Trials: The Story of Davy Crockett's Expedition to the Alamo*. Franklin, TN: Hillsboro Press, 2003.

Crawford, Ann Fears, ed. *The Eagle: The Autobiography of Santa Anna*. Austin, TX: State House Press, 1988.

Crisp, James E. *Sleuthing the Alamo*. New York: Oxford University Press, 2005.

Crockett, David. *Colonel Crockett's Exploits and Adventures in Texas*. New York: William H. Graham, 1848.

——. *Davy Crockett's Own Story as Written by Himself*. Philadelphia: G. G. Evans, 1860.

Curtis, Albert. *Remember the Alamo*. San Antonio: Clegg Company, 1961.

Day, Donald, and Harry Herbert, eds. *Autobiography of Sam Houston*. Norman: University of Oklahoma Press, 1954.

DeShields, James T. *Tall Men with Long Rifles: The Glamour Story of the Texas Revolution as Told by Captain Creed Taylor*. San Antonio: Naylor Printing Company, 1935.

Edmondson, J. R. *The Alamo Story: From Early History to Current Conflicts*. Plano: Republic of Texas Press, 2000.

Flores, Richard R. *Remembering the Alamo: Memory, Modernity, and the Master Symbol*. Austin: University of Texas Press, 2002.

Ford, John S. *Origin and Fall of the Alamo*. San Antonio: Johnson Brothers Printing Company, 1895.

Groneman, Bill. *Death of a Legend: The Myth and Mystery Surrounding the Death of Davy Crockett*. Plano: Republic of Texas Press, 1999.

Hall-Quest, Olga. *Shrine of Liberty: The Alamo*. New York: E. P. Dutton & Company, 1948.

Hardin, Stephen. *The Alamo 1836*. Westport, CT: Praeger, 2004.

Hatch, Thom. *Encyclopedia of the Alamo and the Texas Revolution*. Jefferson, NC: McFarland & Co., 1999.

Hopewell, Clifford. *James Bowie: Texas Fighting Man*. Austin, TX: Eakin Press, 1994.

Houston, Sam. *Letter of General Sam Houston to General Santa Anna, 21 March 1842*. Washington, DC: Congressional Globe Office, 1852.

Huffines, Alan C. *Blood of Noble Men: The Alamo Siege & Battle*. Austin, TX: Eakin Press, 1999.

Jones, Anson. *Valedictory Speech, February 19, 1846, Executive Record Book*. Austin: Texas State Library and Archives Commission.

Kilgore, Dan. *How Did Davy Die?* College Station: Texas A&M University Press, 1978.

King, C. Richard. *James Clinton Neill: The Shadow Commander of the Alamo*. Austin, TX: Eakin Press, 2002.

———. *Susanna Dickinson: Messenger of the Alamo*. Austin, TX: Shoal Creek Publishers, 1976.

Lane, Walter P. *The Adventures and Recollections of General Walter P. Lane, a San Jacinto Veteran*. Marshall, TX: Tri-Weekly Herald Job Print, 1887.

Linn, John J. *Reminiscences of Fifty Years in Texas*. New York: D. & J. Sadlier & Co., 1883.

Long, Jeff. *Duel of Eagles: The Mexican and U.S. Fight for the Alamo*. New York: William Morrow and Company, 1990.

Lord, Walter A. *A Time to Stand*. New York: Harper & Brothers, 1961.

Matovina, Timothy M. *The Alamo Remembered: Tejano Accounts and Perspectives*. Austin: University of Texas Press, 1995.

McAlister, George A. *Alamo: The Price of Freedom*. San Antonio: Docutex, 1988.

McDonald, Archie P. *Travis*. Austin, TX: Jenkins Publishing Co., 1976.

Myers, John M. *The Alamo*. New York: E. P. Dutton & Company, 1948.

Potter, Reuben M. *The Fall of the Alamo*. Hillsdale, NJ: Otterden Press, 1977.

Procter, Ben H. *The Battle of the Alamo*. Austin: Texas State Historical Association, 1986.

Rios, John F., ed. *Readings on the Alamo*. New York: Vantage Press, 1987.

Rogers, Lisa Waller. *A Texas Sampler: Historical Recollections*. Lubbock: Texas Tech University Press, 1998.

Rosenthal, Phil, and Bill Groneman. *Roll Call at the Alamo*. Fort Collins, CO: Old Army Press, 1985.

Sánchez Lamego, Miguel A. *The Siege and Taking of the Alamo*. Santa Fe, NM: Press of the Territorian, 1968.

Santos, Richard G. *Santa Anna's Campaign against Texas*. Waco, TX: Texian Press, 1968.

Scott, Robert J. *After the Alamo*. Plano: Republic of Texas Press, 2000.

Texas State Historical Society. *Handbook of Texas Online*. May 16, 2003. http://www.tsha.utexas.edu/handbook/online/ (June 12, 2007).

Thompson, Frank. *The Alamo: A Cultural History*. Dallas: Taylor Trade Publishing, 2001.

Tinkle, Lon. *13 Days to Glory: The Siege of the Alamo*. College Station: Texas A&M University Press, 1985.

Tomerlin, Jacqueline Beretta, comp. *Fugitive Letters, 1829–1836 Stephen F. Austin to David G. Burnet*. San Antonio: Trinity University Press, 1981.

Turner, Martha Anne. *William Barrett Travis: His Sword and His Pen*. Waco, TX: Texian Press, 1972.

Williams, Amelia W., and Eugene C. Barker, eds. *The Writings of Sam Houston 1813–1863*. Vol.1. Austin, TX: Jenkins Publishing Company, 1970.

Winders, Richard Bruce. *Sacrificed at the Alamo: Tragedy and Triumph in the Texas Revolution*. Abilene, TX: State House Press, 2004.

Wlodarski, Robert. *The Haunted Alamo*. Calabasas, CA: G-Host Publishing, 1996.

FURTHER READING AND WEBSITES

BOOKS

Altsheler, Joseph A. *The Texan Scouts: A Story of the Alamo and Goliad.* New York: Appleton-Century-Crofts, 1941.

Barry, James P. *The Louisiana Purchase, April 30, 1803: Thomas Jefferson Doubles the Area of the Unites States.* New York: Franklin Watts, 1973.

Bredeson, Carmen. *The Battle of the Alamo: The Fight for Texas Territory.* Brookfield, CT: Millbrook Press, 1996.

Caravantes, Peggy. *An American in Texas: The Story of Sam Houston.* Greensboro, NC: Morgan Reynolds Publishing, 2003.

Carter, Alden R. *Last Stand at the Alamo.* New York: F. Watts, 1990.

Craig, David, and Shelley Tanaka. *A Day That Changed America: The Alamo.* New York: Hyperion Books, 2003.

Deem, James M. *Primary Source Accounts of the Mexican-American War.* Berkeley Heights, NJ: MyReportLinks.com Books, 2006.

Edmondson, J. R. *Jim Bowie: Frontier Legend, Alamo Hero.* New York: PowerPlus Books, 2003.

Feldman, Ruth Tenzer. *The Mexican-American War.* Minneapolis: Twenty–First Century Books, 2004.

Fritz, Jean. *Make Way for Sam Houston.* New York: Putnam Juvenile, 1998.

Garland, Sherry. *In the Shadow of the Alamo.* San Diego: Harcourt, 2001.

——. *Voices of the Alamo.* Gretna, LA: Pelican Publishing Company, 2004.

Jakes, John. *Susanna of the Alamo: A True Story.* San Diego: Gulliver Books, 1986.

Kerr, Rita. *Girl of the Alamo: Story of Susanna Dickinson.* Houston: Hendrick-Long Publishing Company, 1984.

——— *The Immortal 32: Thirty-Two Men from Gonzales Answered the Plea from the Alamo.* Houston: Hendrick-Long Publishing Company, 1986.

——. *Juan Seguín Hero of Texas.* San Antonio, TX.: Marion Koogler McNay Art Museum, 1985.

Marrin, Albert. *Empires Lost and Won.* New York: Atheneum, 1997.

Marvin, Isabel R. *One of Fannin's Men: A Survivor at Goliad.* Houston: Hendrick-Long Publishing Company, 1997.

McNeese, Tim. *The Alamo.* New York: Chelsea House, 2003.

Murphy, Jim. *Inside the Alamo.* New York: Delacorte Press, 2003.

Phelan, Mary Kay. *The Story of the Louisiana Purchase.* New York: Crowell, 1979.

Scott, John Anthony. *Hard Trials on My Way; Slavery and the Struggle against It: 1800–1860.* New York: Knopf, 1974.

Silverstein, Herma. *The Alamo.* New York: Dillon Press, 1992.

Sullivan, George. *Davy Crockett.* New York: Scholastic Reference, 2001.

Tanaka, Shelley. *The Alamo: Surrounded and Outnumbered, They Chose to Make a Defiant Last Stand.* New York: Hyperion Books for Children, 2003.

Tolliver, Ruby C. *Santa Anna: Patriot or Scoundrel.* Houston: Hendrick-Long Publishing Company, 1992.

Weber, Valerie J., and Janet Riehecky. *The Siege of the Alamo.* Milwaukee: Gareth Stevens Publishing, 2002.

WEBSITES

The Alamo
> http://www.thealamo.org/main.html
> This is the official Alamo Historic Site Web page, with a history of the site, information on visiting the area, and some educational materials.

American West: The Alamo
> http://www.americanwest.com/pages/alamo.htm
> This site is produced by the Texas State Travel Office, and it includes biographies of many of the personalities involved in the Alamo, along with a list of the defenders who died there, maps, and a timeline.

Daughters of the Republic of Texas Library
> http://www.drtl.org/History/index.asp
> This website of the Daughters of the Republic of Texas Library includes a brief history of the Alamo.

The Handbook of Texas Online
> http://www.tsha.utexas.edu/handbook/online/index.html
> Produced by the Texas State Historical Association and the University of Texas, this is a wonderful, searchable site on Texas history.

The Second Flying Company of Alamo de Parras
> http://www.tamu.edu/ccbn/dewitt/adp/
> Produced by Texas A&M University, this website brings light onto the history of the Alamo, before and after its famous battle, as well as the Texas Revolution. This challenging site includes a glossary, biographies, and book reviews.

Texas State Library and Archives Commission
> http://www.tsl.state.tx.us/ref/abouttx/index.html
> This comprehensive "About Texas" website includes information and links to websites about Texas, including both its past and present.

The Texas Tides Digital Learning Consortium
> http://tides.sfasu.edu/home.html
> This website, started by the Stephen F. Austin State University in Nacogdoches, Texas, provides primary resource materials from and about the Texas region dating back to 1546.

INDEX

French and Indian War, 7

Goliad, 32, 38, 47, 56, 70–78, 79; eye-
    witness accounts of, 74, 75, 77,
    78; massacre at, 70, 74, 75, 77,
    78, 79; as rallying cry, 78, 93;
    revenge for, 83; surrender at,
    72–73; Texian takeover of, 26
Gonzales (town), 26–27
Guadalupe Hidalgo, Treaty of, 92

Handbook of Texas, The, 34
Harris, Dilue Rose, 81, 85
Houston, Sam, 29, 30, 38, 70, 94;
    assessment of the Alamo, 39; as
    commander in chief, 27, 33, 35,
    39, 68–69, 79, 80, 81, 82, 83, 85,
    93; and independence move-
    ment, 40, 84; and Native
    Americans, 39, 40; as president
    of the Republic of Texas, 88, 90,
    91

Illinois, 10
Indiana, 10
Iowa, 11

Jackson, Andrew, 38, 84, 85, 87, 88
Jefferson, Thomas, 12, 13
Joe (Travis's slave), 17, 48, 67
Jones, Anson, 91, 94

Kansas, 11, 14
Kentucky, 10, 11, 34

Lamar, Mirabeau, 90
land grants in Texas, 15, 16, 17, 20,
    24–25
Lane, Walter P., 79, 82, 83
Lewis, Meriwether, 13
Lewis and Clark expedition, 13
Little House on the Prairie, The, 10–11
Louisiana, 11, 34
Louisiana Purchase, 11, 12, 13, 92
Lynch's Ferry, 81

Martínez, Antonio, 16, 17
Mexican–American War, 86, 91, 92

Mexican army, 40, 71, 80; under Cos,
    26–27, 28; under Santa Anna, 6,
    49, 50, 51, 53, 54, 56, 81, 89. *See
    also* soldados
Mexico, 6, 9, 12, 29; government of,
    19, 20, 22, 23, 25, 42, 73, 89, 92;
    rebellions within, 21, 26; as
    republic, 17, 40; response to
    Texas statehood, 90, 91; and
    Spain 15, 16, 17, 40
Mexico City, 16, 25, 28, 41, 49, 91, 92
Millsaps, Isaac, 54
Minnesota, 11
Mississippi, 35
Mississippi River, 14
Missouri, 10, 11, 34
Montana, 11

Native Americans, 13, 14, 15, 21, 39,
    40, 44
Nebraska, 11
Neill, James, 31, 32, 36
Nevada, 12, 92
New France, 15
New Mexico, 11, 12, 92
New Spain, 12, 14–16
North Dakota, 11

Ohio, 10
Oklahoma, 11

Peña, Jose Enrique de la, 64, 68
Polk, James K., 90, 91
Portilla, Nicolás de la, 74, 75
prisoners of war, 72, 73, 83 84; exe-
    cution of, 74–78

"Remember the Alamo," 9, 78, 82, 93
Remington, Frederick, 14
Rio Grande, 91, 92
Rocky Mountains, 11
Roman Catholic faith, 15, 19, 23
Roosevelt, Franklin D., 9
Rose, Louis, 66
Ruiz, Francisco, 48, 59, 68
Runaway Scrape, 80, 81, 85

Saldana, Rafael, 64

About the Author

Susan Provost Beller is the author of twenty history books for young readers. She writes from her home in Charlotte, Vermont, when she is not either traveling to see historic sites or visiting with her three children and five grandchildren. Her one wish is that someone would invent a time machine so she could go back and really see the past!

Photo Acknowledgments

The images in this book are used with the permission of: © Laura Westlund/Independent Picture Service, pp. 1, 2–3 (background), 52, 96, all sidebar backgrounds; © Sandy Felsenthal/CORBIS, p. 2; © Peter Horree/Alamy, p. 7; Library of Congress, pp. 8, 34 (LC-USZ62-119830), 39 (LC-USZ62-110029), 40 (LC-USA62-21276), 61, 62 (LC-USZC4-2133), 71, 75 (LC-USZ62-131347), 85 (LC-USZ62-5099), 89 (LC-DIG-cwpbh-02619), 90 (LC-USZ62-5770); © MPI/Hulton Archive/Getty Images, p. 11; © Bettmann/CORBIS, pp. 12, 19, 27, 41, 44, 66, 94; © Hulton Archive/Getty Images, pp. 13, 14, 37; © Time & Life Pictures/Getty Images, p. 15; © North Wind Picture Archives, pp. 17, 47; Russell Fish III/Texas Memorial Museum, p. 18; © CORBIS, p. 20; © Brown Brothers, pp. 24, 31, 46, 91; Texas State Library and Archives Comission, pp. 28, 32, 38, 77, 82; The State Preservation Board, Austin, Texas, pp. 48, 84; © Culver Pictures, p. 55; Art Resource, NY, p. 60; The New York Public Library/Art Resource, NY, p. 63; AP Photo/John Hayes, p. 65; Daughters of the Republic of Texas, p. 67; San Jacinto Museum of History, p. 75; Peter Newark's American Pictures, p. 88; National Archives, War and Conflict Collection, p. 92; University of Tennessee Library/Special Collections, p. 93.

Cover: © Donne Bryant/Art Resource, NY (main); © Laura Westlund/Independent Picture Service (background).